'Do you expect an apology?'

He was so blatant in his judgement, she had to laugh. 'I wouldn't hold my breath.'

Quinn nodded and smiled to himself, then took her completely by surprise by closing the space between them in two swift strides. One long-fingered hand reached out to cup her chin. Her eyes widened as danger signals went off in her head, urging her to move. But he had outmanoeuvred her and, though she did lift a hand, instead of brushing his hand away her fingers closed about his wrist and held on as a delicious, tingling warmth began to expand from the spot. Her brain seemed to grow sluggish, and her eyelids grew so heavy it took all her energy to stop them from closing. They fluttered.

'You're very good,' he said quietly, and it took a second or two for his meaning to sink in.

Discovering a talent for acting she had previously been unaware of, Laura pulled away, flouncing out of hi___ ___le. 'If ___ ___'t ___ing to buy, don't touch ___ ___'

Amanda Browning still lives in the Essex house where she was born. The third of four children—her sister being her twin—she enjoyed the rough and tumble of life with two brothers as much as she did reading books. Writing came naturally as an outlet for a fertile imagination. The love of books led her to a career in libraries, and being single allowed her to take the leap into writing for a living. Success is still something of a wonder, but allows her to indulge in hobbies as varied as embroidery and bird-watching.

A CHRISTMAS SEDUCTION

BY
AMANDA BROWNING

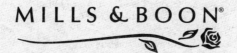

MILLS & BOON®

First published in Great Britain 1998
Harlequin Mills & Boon Limited,
Eton House, 18-24 Paradise Road, Richmond, Surrey TW9 1SR

© Amanda Browning 1998

ISBN 0 263 81318 5

Set in Times Roman 10½ on 12 pt.
01-9812-51727 C1

Printed and bound in Norway
by AIT Trondheim AS, Trondheim

CHAPTER ONE

FROM the moment Laura Maclane met Quinn Mannion, a state of war would exist between them. Not that she knew it that rain-lashed Friday night, as she paid off the taxi and made a dash for the door of the building where Jonathan Ames had his law practice. Jonathan had been Alexander Harrington's lawyer and was the only living soul, apart from herself, who knew about his relationship with her mother, and her own relationship to him. The world at large was still speculating about it but, as yet, nobody had come close to the truth, which was that she was Alexander Harrington's natural daughter.

Laura had never known her father's name. She had had no idea who he was until her mother had died of cancer, leaving instructions that Laura was to inform Alexander Harrington of her death. He had realised at once who she was, but his quite understandable shock had quickly been surpassed by his obvious pleasure. It had been Laura herself who had doubted his claim to parentage, but a blood test had proved he was right. She had the same rare blood group as himself. She was his daughter.

She had known very little about the affair which had brought about her existence. Her mother had never revealed any details. From Alexander she had learned that he and her mother had met at university and fallen in love. They had lived together for a while, but then Alexander's father had died and he had had to return home. There had been problems, and one thing had led to another. He never did go back, and had never seen her mother again. She, for whatever reason, had kept her pregnancy to herself. He had married and raised a family, never knowing he had another child.

Blame was not something Alexander had cared to apportion. He had accepted that he had treated her mother badly, and that withholding knowledge of his child had been her revenge. Fault lay on both sides, but it was in the past. He knew about his daughter now, and he was determined to make up for lost time.

They had spent as much time as they could together over the next few months, getting to know each other. Alexander's wealth and position in life had taken some getting used to, but not for a second had she been envious of it. If she envied anything at all, it was the family she did not know. She had never pushed him to introduce her to her half-brother and sister, though she longed to meet them. Being an only child had been very lonely at times. Alexander, however, had been determined that she should become part of the family one day. The difficulty was telling his wife. She was unaware of her husband's brief affair almost thirty years ago. It was bound to come as a shock, and he wanted to minimise it because Maxine Harrington had a serious heart problem. He would have to pick his time carefully.

Until then they had tried to be discreet, but somehow the ever vigilant press had found out about their meetings. The next thing Laura had known, her picture had appeared in the society gossip columns above a caption asking who was this woman who was constantly seen with the wealthy financier Alexander Harrington? Speculation had been rife. Knowing it would only be a matter of time before somebody actually claimed they must be lovers, Alexander had decided he must act.

However, before he had been able to put the facts right, he had suffered a massive stroke from which he'd never recovered. He had died a few days later, at the age of fifty-one.

That might have been the end of it, except for Alexander's will. Laura had been astounded to discover that he had left her a very great deal of money. When the press got hold of that little snippet, she had been described in various unkind ways, not the least of which was gold-digger. As if she had somehow known he was going to die so suddenly! Sadly, she had accepted it was impossible to put the matter right, at least in the eyes of the press and society. For one thing, nobody would accept a denial at this late stage. For another, she had promised Alexander she would say nothing of their true relationship until he had broken it to his family.

Stymied, that was how things stood several months later. She still secretly hoped to be able to meet her family one day. She just didn't know how to bring it about.

To this day, only Jonathan knew the truth. Because of it, she considered him her best friend. Sometimes it seemed he was her only friend, she thought wryly, brushing droplets of rain off her coat before stepping into the building.

At this time of night the foyer was quiet, and she headed for the bank of elevators to the echoing sound of her own footsteps. She stepped into the nearest and pressed the button for the third floor. The system was old and cranky and progress was slow, and Laura used the time to take a quick glance at her reflection in the mirror, to check for any damage the rain might have caused. There was very little.

Her blonde hair curled under in a shining bob to just

below her ears. It made her heart-shaped face appear all the more fragile. Her grey eyes, with their long lashes, stared back at her doe-like, whilst her surprisingly full mouth was curved in a faint smile. Beneath her woollen coat, the soft curves of her body and the length of her legs were shown to perfection by the lines of her black cocktail dress and stiletto shoes.

She looked good for a twenty-eight-year-old interior designer, she decided, and instantly pulled a wry face. As she had overheard one doyenne of society say only recently, what woman wouldn't, given a fortune to spend in only the best stores?

It was a pretty universal assumption. Any money she had must have come from her 'liaison'. Society matrons ignored the fact that she and her friend Anya Kovacs ran a successful interior design business, which they patronised. In the beginning Laura had feared the worst for their combined welfare but, far from slumping through the supposed scandal, business had boomed. The reason had soon become clear; everyone had hoped to be able to glean some titbit of gossip from her. They had been unlucky. Laura had gritted her teeth and refused to utter a word. Some custom had eventually fallen off, but not to the extent she had expected. What clientele remained was loyal because they produced good work.

The elevator came to a stop and, stepping out of it, she turned left towards Jonathan's office. Light glowed beneath the door and she sighed. He was brilliant at his job but, when he was working on a case, he had a head like a sieve about more mundane things. For instance, tonight he was supposed to have picked her up an hour ago for the opening of a new art exhibition, and then they were to have gone on to dinner. She really should have phoned him earlier, but she had assumed he would remember. More fool her.

Pushing open the door, she discovered Jonathan exactly where she expected, bent over his desk, lost in the depths of a file. His brown hair was endearingly tousled, as if he had raked it constantly, and a cup of cold coffee sat by his elbow with a dehydrated jelly doughnut.

'I thought I'd find you here!' Laura exclaimed wryly, and he looked up with a start.

'Laura? What on earth...?' Jonathan gasped in surprise, then his eyes made a quick inspection of her and she saw light dawn. Clapping a hand to his head, he rose to his feet and came round the desk to her, his expression ruefully apologetic. 'Oh, Lord, I'm sorry. We were supposed to be going to the opening, weren't we?' He kissed her cheek and Laura sighed.

'We were,' she confirmed as she raised her hand to brush his hair off his forehead. 'Honestly, you're hopeless. What happened this time?'

'I'm afraid I happened.' A strange voice, rich and slightly husky, broke into their conversation, and it was her turn to jump. She turned towards the voice, but its owner stood in the doorway of Jonathan's private washroom, and the light coming from behind made him little more than a large silhouette.

'Who are you?' she asked more sharply than she intended, and behind her Jonathan shifted uneasily.

'Oh, hell, it had to happen some time, I guess,' he said heavily, and made the introduction. 'This is Quinn.'

Laura went absolutely still, 'Did you say Quinn?' she asked, though she had heard well enough.

'Uh-huh'

Laura had heard a great deal about Alexander's godson, Quinn Mannion. Mentally she recapped what she knew. He was thirty-six years old, a former investigative journalist who now wrote political thrillers which had put him on the top of the best-seller list countless times, and earned him millions of dollars. In the best tradition of novelists he lived in splendid isolation, somewhere on the coast of Maine. Over the years his name had been linked romantically with several women, but he had resisted the ties of marriage. She was curious to know what he looked like, and waited with bated breath as he stepped forward into the light of the desk lamp.

Laura's eyes widened. *This* was Quinn Mannion?

She saw a tall, dark-haired man, broad-shouldered and lean-hipped, wearing a leather jacket over an Aran sweater and jeans he must have been poured into, they hugged his thighs so lovingly. He carried himself with an assurance and self-belief which was almost palpable. Her gaze skittered over his face. He was breathtakingly handsome, although there was nothing soft in it. In fact, the only feature to break the strong lines was a surprisingly sensual mouth. At least, that was what she thought until her eyes met a pair of intense blue ones and somehow got locked there.

They had to be the bluest eyes she had ever seen. The sort of eyes you could dive into and drown in with the greatest pleasure. Rimmed with long dark lashes, they should have been feminine, but weren't. Everything simply made him look even more heart-stoppingly masculine. Quinn Mannion was pretty potent stuff, and deep inside her something elemental stirred. She became, in an instant, so supremely aware of him that every single nerve in her body came to life, tingling in a state of intense receptivity. She knew she would know he was in the same room as her even if she were blindfolded.

It was a disturbingly unfamiliar sensation for her.

Whilst she had always appreciated an attractive man, she had never before been made quite so aware of another human being. Her heart gave a sudden lurch and sprinted away as she recognised what was happening; female recognising the male. This was sexual attraction at its rawest, and the strength of it caused her to breathe in sharply as her stomach clenched on a primitive wave of desire.

More than a little stunned, she remained transfixed, like a rabbit caught in the headlights of a car, as Quinn Mannion advanced on her with a darkling glint in his eye. He came to a halt mere feet away and stared down at her.

'Well, well. As I live and breathe, Laura Maclane in the flesh. The newspaper pictures hardly do you justice,' he drawled disdainfully.

It was a voice which, despite its unfriendliness, conjured up visions of rich dark chocolate. Sinful, luscious and infinitely addictive. Laura fought down a shiver of pure reaction to it.

'Tell me, Laura. Are you enjoying the fruits of your labour?'

The unexpected question set her back on her heels momentarily. She had been prepared to offer a polite greeting for, in a roundabout way, this man was connected to her, but it took only those few words to make her realise there was to be no pretence of pleasantries from him. It wounded her, as all injustice did, but it angered her too. So that was how it was to be, she thought. Well, she could handle anything he cared to throw at her. For instance, that question wasn't an idle one and, though she suspected she wouldn't like the answer, she wasn't about to avoid asking for clarification. She needed to know exactly where she stood with him.

'Labour?'

Quinn's eyes dropped to her mouth and traced the line of her lips with blatant suggestion, so that she had a pretty good idea of what he was going to say before he said it. 'The hard work you put in between the sheets with a man old enough to be your father,' he explained dispassionately, which made the remark all the more insulting.

'Quinn!' Jonathan stepped in warningly, frowning heavily at his friend, but Laura held up her hand. She didn't need protecting, although the words stung. He had no idea how close to the truth he was.

'It's OK, Jonathan. Mr Mannion is saying no more than has been said behind my back. In fact, I give him credit for saying it to my face. The answer to your question is yes. I do enjoy the fruits of my labour,' she confirmed with an unrepentant tilt to her head. Though he didn't know it, she was referring to her business, not her supposed relationship with his godfather.

He did not care for her response. 'I never expected you to be so honest,' he retorted coldly, and she smiled with grim satisfaction. It was the first time she had ever been able to strike a blow for herself since Alexander's death. She discovered that putting noses out of joint, especially this one, could give her quite a kick, and it had the double advantage of taking her mind off her reaction to him. His closeness was setting all her nerves at attention and, under the circumstances, that was treachery of the highest order.

'Oh, I'm full of surprises,' she retorted mockingly, finding it remarkably easy to slip into the character he thought her. For months she had had to hold her tongue, and the relief of verbal battle was quite heady. If he wanted a fight, she would give him one. In spades.

He smiled then, and he reminded her of nothing so much as a tiger—a very hungry one. 'I just bet you are. As a matter of interest, just how did you manage to snare him? I would have expected someone of Alex's intelligence to see you coming.'

Laura ground her teeth. Lord, when this man went for the jugular, he held nothing back. 'Do you want the gory details, or will a rough outline do?' she asked sweetly, all the while sending invisible daggers into him.

Quinn's lips twitched, though the amusement was chilly. 'I'm a big boy. You don't have to spare my blushes.'

'I doubt very much that you have ever blushed, Mr Mannion,' she returned pithily.

'Quinn,' he invited, swatting her verbal dart aside and returning one of his own.

Committing murder had never been so inviting a proposition. 'Are you sure we're on intimate enough terms for Christian names?' she asked coyly, and he laughed dryly.

'Rest assured you and I will never be on intimate terms but I think, under the circumstances, we can dispense with the formality.'

So, they were to play games, were they? That was fine by her, too.

Laura allowed a sensual smile to spread across her lips. 'Quinn, then,' she flirted dangerously, and from the corner of her eye caught sight of the stunned expression on Jonathan's face.

'Don't do this, Laura,' he advised urgently, knowing full well that Quinn was a formidable opponent and never backed away from a fight but, before he could do more to head her off, his friend was responding.

'He's right. It wouldn't be a wise move to use your feminine wiles on me, Laura.'

Ignoring the look on Jonathan's face, Laura ventured where angels and sensible folk feared to tread. 'Why not? It could be fun,' she teased, boldly reaching out to run her fingers up and down the zip of his jacket, wondering at the same time just exactly where it was she got her nerve.

With a look of distaste, Quinn brushed her hand away. 'Believe me, you wouldn't enjoy the experience,' he warned, but, truth be told, she was beginning to enjoy herself and merely batted her lashes at him.

'You don't know what I like,' she purred sultrily.

His beautiful mouth twisted into a sneer. 'I'm beginning to get the picture. Now cut it out.'

Delighted by her success, Laura heaved an elaborate sigh, as if to say he was no fun. 'All right, where was I?'

'You were about to tell me the truth about how you got my godfather to give you all that money,' Quinn gritted through his teeth.

Actually, that was the very last thing she was about to do. She had a deep dislike of people who jumped to conclusions. He knew nothing of her, save what he had obviously read in the newspapers, and he had already decided it was true. Since he had clearly made up his mind, she was not going to waste time trying to persuade him differently.

'I used the gifts God gave me,' she vouchsafed provocatively, and it didn't surprise her in the least to see his gaze travel the length of her body. Quinn Mannion was nothing if not predictable.

'With which you are fulsomely endowed,' he drawled

contemptuously, making her blood boil. 'I never thought my godfather would be so easily taken in.'

Unabashed, she smiled. 'Alexander got exactly what he wanted from me. Do you want me to draw you a picture?' she challenged sweetly. It was amazingly easy to dislike this man, even if he did have megawatt sex appeal which turned her insides to mush.

'I'll pass, thanks.'

He looked as if he had just discovered a bad smell right under his nose, and Laura couldn't resist taunting him some more, to rub salt in the wound.

'We were about to go to dinner. Would you care to join us?' she invited, and heard Jonathan's sharp intake of breath. He was going to be livid.

'Sorry, but I can't.' Quinn refused with every appearance of regret. 'There's someplace I have to be and—' he glanced at the gold Rolex on his wrist '—I'm late already.'

Her smile of dismay was as sincere as his regret. 'What a shame. Another time, perhaps?' she ventured politely, holding out her hand. Unable to be so pointedly rude as to ignore her gesture, Quinn reached across and took it.

His hand closed around hers. Flesh touched flesh, and it seemed to Laura that a breathtakingly powerful charge of electricity shot clean through her system, bringing every atom of her body alive. It was like being plugged into a live socket. Her heartbeat accelerated off the scale, and her blood ran hot and thick through her veins so that her whole body thrummed with it. It was a totally stunning sensation.

When Quinn released her and turned to Jonathan, Laura was left trembling in the aftershock. She had never felt so unnerved in her life. An hour ago she had been in blissful ignorance of the possibilities, but now she was seriously rattled. She was left gazing down at a still tingling palm. She drew in a shaky breath. My God, she thought dazedly, how could a simple touch do that?

'What on earth did you think you were doing?' Jonathan snapped at her, bringing her head up sharply. They were alone. Quinn had gone.

'What?' she asked blankly, still rocked by her reaction. She could scarcely believe it had happened, yet her hand told her it most certainly had. She shivered. She was glad he was gone. If she never saw him again, it would be too soon.

Jonathan raked an agitated hand through his hair. 'My God, Laura, you were acting like an idiot!' he exclaimed in disbelief.

'I was acting the way he expected me to act,' she declared defensively, and Jonathan rolled his eyes heavenwards, seeking patience.

'You could have disappointed him.'

Laura was fully aware that she had just done herself no favours, but the man had rubbed her up the wrong way right from the beginning and she did not regret what she had done. In fact she would do it again, with as much satisfaction.

'His assumption annoyed me,' she pointed out testily, and he snorted.

'You don't say!'

She frowned at him. 'There's no need to be sarcastic. You know very well I couldn't tell him the truth,' she argued reasonably.

Jonathan jammed his hands in his pockets as if to keep from strangling her. 'Maybe not, but you didn't have to tell such a bald-faced lie, either.'

Her still tingling palm was annoying her, and she rubbed it over her coat to ease it. 'I didn't say a thing!' she protested, and he laughed humourlessly.

'Trust me, your implications were eloquent. Quinn now thinks you're the very worst kind of gold-digger.'

'I wasn't aware there was any good kind of gold-digger,' she riposted facetiously, and drew a quelling look for her pains.

'Laura...!'

She held up her hands in defeat. 'Oh, all right, I admit I was at fault. I just couldn't help myself. It was either that or punch him on the nose.'

That finally brought a smile to Jonathan's pursed mouth. 'All in all, I think I'd rather you'd hit him,' he admitted drolly.

Laura laughed, but soon sobered again. 'What was he doing here, anyway? It gave me the shock of my life to find him with you.' Although she knew of all the close members of Alexander's family, and had hoped to meet them, she had never expected to do so in such a fashion.

Jonathan moved away and began clearing up his desk. 'Actually, he was delivering a message from Maxine,' he informed her, mentioning Alexander's wife.

'That must have been nice for you,' she said dryly, and Jonathan shot her a mildly reproving look. 'Sorry,' she apologised quickly, knowing her response had been left over from her run-in with Quinn. She had no reason to dislike Maxine Harrington.

'I happen to be a close friend of the family and, as such, I was being invited to spend Christmas with them in the usual way.'

Her surprise was genuine. 'I had no idea you knew the family that well.'

'As it happens, the law firm of Ames and Ames have

been legal advisers to the Harrington family for several generations. Christmas has become something of a tradition. I could hardly refuse,' he said apologetically, as if she would think it disloyal of him.

'No, of course not,' she concurred readily. 'I don't imagine it will be much fun this year.'

'Grim would be the word I'd choose to describe it. It will be the first holiday without Alexander. Speaking of which, you know that Philip and Stella wanted to contest the will?'

'No! How could they?' The suggestion that Alexander had been in less than full control of his faculties made her mad enough to spit nails. 'What about Maxine?'

Jonathan smiled at her angry tone. She sounded like a she-bear defending her cubs. Alexander would have been pleased to know he had one of his staunchest defenders in the guise of his eldest daughter.

'She would have none of it. Maxine is a very classy lady. She might resent like hell who she thinks you are, but if Alexander wanted to leave you money she is not about to challenge it. You'd like her.'

Laura let out a puff of air and relaxed again. 'I want to like them all. I want to know them all. They're my family, but how can I tell them? I can't baldly come out with it. For heaven's sake, the shock could kill her and then where would I be? Everything is such a mess.'

'I agree, but the time will come when you can tell them.'

Laura shook her head, her eyes filling as they had a habit of doing whenever she thought about Alexander. She was constantly surprised by how much she missed her father, when she'd hardly known him. 'He was a good man, wasn't he?'

'One of the best,' Jonathan agreed, slipping an arm about her shoulders and giving her a hug.

Laura made a determined effort to chase the blues away. 'I seem to remember Alexander telling me that the family always spend Christmas at the house in Vermont.'

'That's right. We all travel up a day or two before Christmas and stay until New Year,' Jonathan confirmed.

She sighed. A genuine family gathering. She would have given a lot to be there. As a child she had always longed to be part of a large family, but there had been only herself and her mother. She had thought it might be different this year, but with Alexander gone... She was on her own again.

'I don't suppose you're allowed to bring a guest, are you?' she asked wistfully, then caught her breath as an audacious idea came to her out of the blue.

'I could if I wanted,' he acknowledged cautiously, something in her expression making him distinctly uneasy. 'Why do you ask?'

'Dare I?' Laura asked herself out loud, still lost in thought.

'Dare you what? Why am I beginning to feel very uneasy?' Jonathan muttered dryly, and she grimaced.

'Probably because you're getting to know me too well,' she quipped, then, taking the bull by the horns, sent him a beguiling smile. 'I really do want to meet them, Jonathan,' she said huskily.

Jonathan suddenly felt like a man on the way to his own execution. 'What exactly are you suggesting?'

She took a deep breath, then blurted it out. 'How would you like some friendly company for Christmas?'

He blinked. 'You're not serious!'

'I wouldn't say a word, honestly,' she insisted, intent on persuasion. 'All I want to do is get to know them, and give them a chance to get to know me.''

Jonathan held up his hands to ward her off. 'Oh, no. No way!'

'Please!' she begged. 'I'll be good. You'll never know I'm there!'

He dragged a hand through his hair. 'It's not me I'm worried about. The family won't like it,' he warned.

She bit her lip. He had a point. Yet she knew she had to do this. 'They can hardly turn me away if I'm with you,' she declared, though she wasn't entirely sure if that was true.

'True, but… Good Lord, Laura, have you considered everything? It won't be pleasant for you.'

Laura shrugged that off, warming to the idea more and more. If she could just get them to see she wasn't some sort of monster, they might be more receptive to the facts she hoped to tell them. Besides, she would be better able to gauge Maxine's possible reaction. Was it really so much to ask?

'I know it, but I can take anything they throw at me.'

Jonathan shook his head. 'I've got to be out of my mind,' he murmured, and the oblique agreement made Laura fling her arms around him.

'Oh, thank you. You're a wonderful man.'

'Don't overdo it,' he advised, and shook his head again. 'I know I'm going to live to regret this.'

'No, you aren't. This is the opportunity we've been waiting for. When are they expecting you?'

'Next Wednesday evening,' he revealed, and tried one last time to dissuade her. 'Are you sure you're doing the right thing?'

Laura pressed a hand over her anxiously beating heart. 'No, but I'm going to do it anyway.'

Realising she was not about to change her mind, Jonathan bowed to the inevitable. 'I'll pick you up at your apartment around seven.'

'You're not going to tell them I'm coming, are you?' she asked as the thought struck her, but Jonathan shook his head.

'I think I'd prefer to surprise them. They might shoot the messenger for bringing bad news,' he told her dryly, rounding his desk and locking away in a drawer the file he had been reading. 'Are you ready for supper now?' Collecting his overcoat from the stand by the door, he draped it over his arm.

'Won't our table have gone?' Laura reminded him, but he grinned.

'Nope. I remembered what happened the last time I took you to an opening and ordered the table for an hour later. If we hurry we should just about make it,' he revealed, taking her arm and guiding her from the office.

'My, what a clever boy you are!'

'If I was that clever, I wouldn't be letting you persuade me to set the cat among the pigeons.'

'I'm a very docile cat,' Laura murmured sweetly.

'Hmm. Tell that to the pigeons!'

CHAPTER TWO

'Warm enough?'

Laura sighed and stretched her toes towards the warm air coming from the heater. The car was a luxury model. Jonathan never drove anything but the best.

'Mmm. It's sending me to sleep,' she murmured. It had been a long day, and the traffic leaving the city for the holiday season had made it seem endless. They had left it behind now, though, and progress was quicker.

'Why don't you nap for a while? We've still got some way to go,' Jonathan suggested, sparing her a glance which brought a smile to his lips, before concentrating once more on his driving.

Laura liked the sound of that. She hadn't slept much the previous night for thinking of the visit ahead of her. Not that she regretted her decision to come. She didn't. However, she knew it wasn't going to be pleasant walking into a place where she knew she wasn't wanted. Consequently she had slept only fitfully, and now her eyes felt gritty from lack of sleep.

'You'd better wake me before we get there. I don't want to turn up looking like something the cat dragged in,' she drawled wryly, making herself as comfortable as the seat belt would allow.

'You never look anything less than lovely to me,' Jonathan responded gallantly, and she smiled without opening her eyes.

'You always say the right thing. It's a wonder some woman hasn't snapped you up before now.'

There was an infinitesimal pause before he responded. 'All the best women are already taken,' he said flatly, and Laura heard the soft sigh which followed. She didn't look at him, but rather belatedly she did begin to wonder about Jonathan's love life. Could he be in love with somebody who was married to somebody else? The thought saddened her, for if that was so he was doomed to unhappiness.

'Uh-oh!'

The muffled exclamation brought her eyes open again, in time to see the first snowflakes begin to fall. She sat up, forgetting all about sleep.

'It's snowing!' she cried in delight.

Jonathan snorted. 'Just what we needed,' he said grumpily. He had never made any attempt to hide his dislike of driving in wintry conditions.

'I love snow. It makes everything look clean, bright and magical.'

He rubbed at the windscreen. 'You wouldn't think it so wonderful if you got snowed in.'

Laura laughed ruefully. 'Probably not, but the child in me refuses to think of frozen pipes and no electricity.'

'Perhaps you should move here. There's no shortage of snow in Vermont in winter.'

Laura sat back with a sigh. 'Strange, I always wanted to see Vermont, but I never imagined visiting under these circumstances. It's funny how things turn out.'

'Hilarious.'

'Don't be a grouch,' she reproved lightly. 'Tell me who else will be there besides us.' It would be as well to know beforehand.

'Did anyone ever tell you you're a nag?' he complained before complying with her request. 'Let me see... Besides Maxine there will be Stella and her hus-

band Ian Nevin. Then Philip and his latest girlfriend,'
Jonathan enlarged for her. 'Oh, and Quinn, of course.'

Quinn? Her heart executed a crazy lurch, and her
mouth suddenly became a parched desert. Alarm shot
through her. She hadn't expected him to be one of the
party. Her mind flew back to those dizzying few seconds
when he had touched her hand, and she shivered. The
sensation which had ripped its way through her had been
incredible. The sheer intensity of it was still shocking in
retrospect, so that she hadn't been able to forget it. She
hadn't been able to forget him, either. Much to her chagrin.

He kept slipping into her mind at the most inconven-
ient times. The damned man seemed intent on proving
the adage: once seen, never forgotten. It was driving her
crazy. She swore he was haunting her. His name popped
out of the newspaper every time she opened one, and
just that morning she had seen a tall, rugged man wearing an Aran sweater walk into the studio and, for one
electrifying moment, she had actually thought it was
him! When it turned out to be a complete stranger, her
sense of disappointment had come as an unpleasant
shock. She had had to tell herself quite categorically that
she did not want to see him before she could relax again.

Now, apparently, he was to be at the house for the
holiday, and the knowledge took the bottom out of her
stomach. She groaned. This was ridiculous. Of all the
juvenile reactions! Especially as she despised the man.
She really had to get a grip.

'Why "of course"?' she asked a few minutes later
and Jonathan frowned, not taking his eyes from the road
where the snow was beginning to settle.

'What was that?'

'Why did you say Quinn will be there "of course"?'

she repeated calmly, though her pulse rate was anything but calm.

'Because he always spends Christmas with the family.'

Now he told her. 'Another tradition?' she enquired dryly.

'He and his sister are Alex's godchildren. Quinn loved your father, Laura. Dislike him as much as you want, but never doubt that.'

She would have liked to, considering his opinion of her, but honesty forbade it. She accepted that Quinn Mannion had one good point. He also had the ability to set her senses whirling like dervishes, even *in absentia*. It didn't seem to matter that she disliked the man. Her skin actually prickled with anticipation. Face it, Laura, she told herself sardonically, you're attracted to him. You react to him as you have to no other man.

It wasn't a comforting thought.

Yet she was going to have to live with it. It was either that or cancel the trip. She wondered what Jonathan would say if she asked him to take her back. Nothing printable, of that she could be certain, when she had made such an effort to persuade him to bring her in the first place. Anyway, it wasn't a genuine option. She was not going to turn tail simply because some man was able to light her up like a Christmas tree. She was going to meet her family, and nobody was going to stop her. Especially not Quinn Mannion.

The snow began to fall more heavily as the journey progressed and Laura was glad when, half an hour later, Jonathan turned the car into a gravel driveway and brought it to a halt beside several other vehicles already parked there. She glanced out of the window and her lips parted in pleasure at the sight which met her eyes.

It was almost as if they had wandered into one of those glass snow globes. As if someone had just shaken it, the snow was falling over a gabled house which glittered with frost and fairy lights whilst, from inside, house lights issued a welcoming golden glow.

'It's beautiful,' she breathed.

'I thought you'd appreciate it,' Jonathan declared with a smile.

Somebody must have been on the lookout for their arrival, because by the time Laura had climbed out of the car the front door was open. A young woman of about her own age, and two children, stood silhouetted in the doorway. A muffled sound from beside her brought her attention to Jonathan, who had frozen on the spot and was staring tensely at the house.

'What's wrong?' she asked and, when he didn't answer, followed his gaze back to the small group. 'Who are they?'

Jonathan took a deep breath. 'Quinn's sister Caroline and her two children. She was widowed a couple of years ago. I had no idea they would be here. You go on ahead and I'll bring in the cases.'

There was a tone in his voice which warned her not to ask questions and, respecting it, Laura obediently made her way to the house. Her mind was whirring. Could this be the woman he was in love with? It didn't seem in the least absurd as she climbed the steps and saw just how lovely the woman was. She was clearly surprised by Laura's presence but, even so, her smile was cautiously welcoming.

'Hello, I'm Caroline Stevens, and these two terrors are Tom and Ellie.' Tom, Laura guessed, was about six, and Ellie four. 'I'm sorry, I don't know your name. Jon never mentioned he was bringing a guest. Come inside. Let me take your coat.'

She urged Laura into the warmth of the house and helped her off with her coat. Laura watched as she hung it in the closet, very much aware that, for all the other woman's friendliness, she was struggling to be polite. It occurred to her that Caroline Stevens hadn't expected Jonathan to bring a woman with him, and was surprised to find herself upset by it. Perhaps Jonathan's feelings weren't unreciprocated after all.

'What the hell are you doing here?'

That never-to-be-forgotten voice set the fine hairs all over Laura's body on end. She turned towards the stairs where the owner of it stood on the half-landing. Against her will, the sheer masculine appeal of him took her breath away. Damn it, she thought as her knees showed a tendency to go disastrously weak, why on earth did this have to be happening to her now? It didn't seem to matter to her senses that he was glaring at her, and that she actively disliked him; she was responding to the unseen signals he was putting out. It was that left-over animal instinct. Nature was telling her receptive hormones that here was an ideal male with which to make sure of the continuation of the species. Well, she had news for Mother Nature. The man was far from ideal, and she had no intentions of getting within a good country mile of procreation!

'And good evening to you too, Quinn,' she greeted him blithely, and he descended the last few stairs in no time at all.

'Never mind that. Just give me a straight answer,' he commanded imperiously, and his sister hastily stepped forward.

'Quinn, for heaven's sake! She's a guest!' She remonstrated with him, but he met that with a snort of derision.

'Laura Maclane is no guest in this house,' he returned shortly, and the other woman's eyes grew round as saucers.

'Laura Maclane? Oh…!' She stared at Laura as if she had suddenly grown horns.

'Is she the witch lady Stella talked about?' Tom's young voice piped up, and Laura caught her breath in dismay.

She didn't think 'witch' was the term her half-sister had used but, whatever word it had been, she found it hurt to be spoken of that way. And when Laura was hurt she got angry. How dared Stella talk about her in front of the children? It was inexcusable!

Their mother clearly thought so too. 'Goodness, Tom, what a thing to say!' Caroline exclaimed in embarrassment. 'I must apologise for my son; he had no idea he was being rude.'

Tom frowned heavily, taking exception to the rebuke. 'Uncle Quinn didn't tell Stella off when she said it to him!' he complained, and his mother's colour deepened.

'That's quite enough, young man,' she ordered in a choked voice, only to hear her daughter put in her ten cents' worth.

'Is she really a witch, Mama?' Ellie asked in a quavering voice, and Laura realised the tot was close to being really scared.

Cursing her insensitive half-sister, Laura quickly set about allaying her fears. 'Of course I'm not, sweetheart,' she responded, squatting down so that she could smile directly into the little girl's eyes. 'But I think your uncle and I are about to exchange words, so perhaps it would be better if you went inside, hmm?' she suggested gently, not wanting to alarm her further. Rising, she looked pointedly at Caroline who, after a momentary hesitation, caught her children by the hand and led them away.

Once they were gone, Laura turned to her protagonist.

'Have you been telling tales about me, Quinn, darling?' she drawled sweetly, whilst her eyes shot daggers at him. His own eyes took on a sardonic gleam.

'I don't need to. Your reputation goes before you. This is the last place you should look to for friends.'

'I'm aware of that,' she snapped. It was why she was here, so she could change the way they thought about her. 'I'm angry that somebody's been talking in front of the children. That is unforgivable!' she responded hotly.

'I agree, which was why I put a stop to it,' Quinn replied reasonably, promptly taking the wind out of her sails.

Disconcerted, she eyed him suspiciously. 'You did?'

Quinn nodded in assent. 'As soon as I realised what Stella was doing. Clearly I was too late for some of it.'

'Oh.' Darn it. She did not want to be grateful to this man for anything.

'I can see you're overwhelmed with gratitude,' he observed laconically, and she scowled.

'Stella ought to know that little pitchers have big ears,' she rejoined huffily, refusing to do what he wanted and thank him. The words would choke her.

'She knows now,' Quinn asserted firmly. 'She won't be doing it again.'

In a dizzying about-face, Laura instantly felt sympathy for Stella. 'I bet she loved that! Do you always expect everyone to do what you want?'

The faintest hint of a mocking smile twitched at his lips. 'Let's just say I'm dangerous to cross.'

Laura raised an eyebrow in a gesture less than impressed. 'So is the street outside my studio, but I do it all the time.'

The statement produced another smile. 'Am I supposed to take that as a challenge?' he enquired mildly, and Laura was reminded that a crocodile appeared to smile just before it bit your hand off.

'Do I look like a fool?'

'Actually, no, but that can be deceptive. Looking at you, who would have thought you would sleep your way into a fortune?' he remarked sardonically, and she felt her palm itch with a violent need to slap him hard.

Quinn Mannion had made up his mind about her before they had ever met. As far as he was concerned, the only thing she could have wanted from Alexander was money, and the only way to get it was with sex. What that said of his opinion of his godfather made her furious. Under the circumstances she had no qualms about responding in the provocative way he so disliked.

'Oh, but I didn't sleep. That wouldn't have got me anywhere,' she retorted silkily, and was immensely gratified to see she had indeed got under his skin.

'You have no shame, do you?'

Her smile was as unrepentant as she could possibly make it. 'None at all where Alexander is concerned.'

Quinn shook his head in reluctant admiration at her nerve. 'It's hard to know whether to call you brave or foolhardy. You almost defy description. So what does bring you here? Other than the need to flaunt your victory in the face of the family?'

Tipping her head to one side, Laura let her lips curve lazily. 'Perhaps I simply wanted to see your fabulous blue eyes again. Did you know they look stunning when you're angry?' she taunted and, the funny thing was, it was quite true. Even sending out frosty messages, they were the most amazing eyes she had ever seen.

A strange expression flitted in and out of those blue depths as he went quite still. 'Why are you coming on to me, Laura Maclane?' he asked with disquieting softness, sending a trickle of unease down her spine.

Bearding the lion was a risky business, and probably not the wisest move she could have made under the circumstances. As a rule, her instinct for self-preservation would have made her back off, but not with this man. Unable to resist the impulse to drive a further dart under his skin, she sent him a sultry look from under her lashes and reached out to brush an imaginary speck of fluff off his Argyle sweater.

'Why do you think?' she returned audaciously, and almost leapt out of her skin when his hand snaked out and closed tightly about her wrist. She winced and had to bite down hard on her lip to keep from crying out. 'Brute!'

'I've warned you about playing games. I'm not my godfather. I am neither kind nor a fool. If you've come here to cause trouble, I can give you more trouble than you can imagine. Do you want to think again, *darling?*'

Of all the... If he thought he could get away with manhandling her, he was wrong. Laura was winding up to give him a strong piece of her mind when a sound at the door made them both turn.

'What's going on here?' Jonathan asked sharply as he came in with their cases. Setting them aside, he closed the door and frowned at Quinn who slowly let Laura go.

'So she came here with you, did she?' he observed evenly, as Jonathan disposed of his own coat.

'Do you have a problem with that?' Turning from the

closet, Jonathan crossed to Laura's side and slipped an arm around her shoulder in a purely protective attitude.

Quinn eyed the gesture speculatively. 'I'm wondering if you're out of your mind. Bringing her here is the last thing everyone needs.'

'It doesn't alter the fact that Laura is my guest, and as such has a perfect right to be here,' Jonathan argued, not in the least daunted by Quinn's frosty response.

'I wanted to see the house,' Laura added expansively, not to be outdone. 'When Jonathan told me he was coming here for Christmas, I knew it was the perfect time for me to come too.'

'Even though you know you're not wanted here?' Quinn charged coldly.

Laura winced inwardly as that jibe found its mark. She knew she wasn't wanted, but she hoped to change that. If it meant putting up with this man, she would do it.

'I have a very thick skin,' she lied, looking him squarely in the eye and daring him to say more.

Quinn gave them both long looks, then shrugged as if to say he had done his best. 'Very well, if you're determined to stay I can't stop you, but I'm warning you now, Laura. If you upset anyone, you'll have me to answer to. Do you hear me?'

'I should imagine everyone can hear you,' she replied with dismissive irony. 'By the way, what will you do if someone upsets me?'

He sent her an old-fashioned. 'Somehow, I seriously doubt that will happen.'

She couldn't help but laugh, though her dislike of him was increasing by leaps and bounds. 'You have me all worked out, don't you?' she charged, and he nodded, his eyes glinting mockingly.

'Right down to the last dot so, if you're wise, you'll be very careful and walk softly.' With which piece of advice, he turned his back on the pair of them and disappeared into the lounge.

Laura let out a soundless whistle. 'Wow!'

'Ditto,' Jonathan drawled wryly.

'I don't think he likes me,' she declared with a satisfied smile. The more he disliked her, the more she liked it.

'I can tell you're bothered.'

She laughed grimly. 'Quinn Mannion needs taking down a peg or two. Did you see how easily he believed everything I said? Incredible!'

'What I saw was you playing with fire. He's not the sort of man to make an enemy of, Laura.'

He was already her enemy. 'Don't worry about me. I'll be fine. Besides, nobody's going to run me off. Especially not Quinn Mannion!'

Jonathan gave her a worried look. 'Seriously, Laura. I wouldn't tangle with him if I were you. He doesn't believe in losing,' he cautioned like the good friend he was.

Losing wasn't on her agenda, either, she thought determinedly. 'I'm only going to play with him a little.' Just enough to really irritate him. She would be the nuisance fly he just couldn't swat.

Jonathan look at her unhappily. 'I've got a bad feeling about this, but I don't suppose that's going to change your mind, is it?' he asked as he took her by the elbow and turned her towards the door Quinn had disappeared through.

'Not in the least,' she agreed determinedly. 'Oh, by the way, I liked the look of your Caroline,' she added gently, and wasn't in the least surprised to see a tide of warm colour wash into his cheeks. Aha. So she was getting warm.

'She's not my Caroline,' Jonathan denied, and Laura smiled sympathetically.

'Really? Then why did I get the impression she might like to be? She was very put out to see me arriving with you, and that was before she knew who I was,' she told him, and felt her heart twist at the sudden hope she saw in his eyes.

'She was?' he asked with such boyish eagerness it quite made her envious.

Laura slipped her arm through his and gave it a squeeze. 'Oh, yes. I think it might not be quite as hopeless as you imagine.' She hoped she was right. One look at Caroline Stevens had convinced her that she was just the sort of woman Jonathan needed.

The sound of raised voices greeted them as they approached the doorway to the lounge, and Laura braced herself for their entry into the room.

'Mother, you cannot have that woman in this house!' a female voice declared in outrage. 'You can't let her insult you so!'

'Oh, Stella, darling, do keep your voice down. She'll hear you,' a gentler voice implored softly.

'I don't care if she does! Quinn should have seen her off at once!' the younger voice declared unrepentantly.

Just as if I were a beggar, Laura thought desolately, trying not to be hurt but feeling it all the same. Was it naive to expect these people to like her? Wasn't she just asking for trouble? Maybe, but she was committed now. She had to go on.

They stepped inside just as Stella Nevin dropped back into her chair. Everyone turned to look at them.

'Stop being such a brat, Stella,' the man seated at her

side rebuked her. 'I apologise for my wife's childish behaviour,' he added, and Laura realised he must be Ian Nevin.

She had never lacked courage but, in all honesty, she hadn't expected it to be quite so difficult to walk in there. There was a distinctly uncomfortable atmosphere in the room, and she knew it was due to her presence. She quickly took stock of the occupants. She recognised Maxine and her two children from the photographs Alexander had had of them, and of course Stella's husband. The only other occupant besides Quinn, his sister and her children was Philip's girlfriend. A tiny brown mouse of a girl who looked as if she wouldn't say boo to a goose.

Not so Stella. She had every intention of having her opinion heard. 'Don't apologise to her,' she declared, affronted. 'Why, she's nothing but a...a...'

Fortunately, Stella's reaction was just the goad Laura needed to bolster her nerve. 'Gold-digger appears to be the description of choice.' She helped her out as she strolled into the room with every appearance of calm. Hopefully nobody would realise she was faking it.

Colour stormed into her half-sister's pretty face, but her chin went up. 'Gold-digger, then!' she repeated, and Laura couldn't help but laugh, for she knew that look. It had graced her own face countless times as she was growing up. Laughter eased her tension wonderfully.

'Bravo,' she applauded, and Stella frowned at her in sudden confusion.

Turning away from her half-sister, Laura took a deep breath and squared her shoulders as she walked over to where Maxine Harrington sat in a chair by the fire. She was an elegant if frail-looking woman who had never been beautiful, but had a presence that age could not dim.

Laura held out her hand. 'How do you do, Mrs Harrington? I'm very pleased to meet you at last,' she said pleasantly, determined that she, at least, would show good manners, whatever reception she received.

Maxine Harrington looked from the outstretched hand to Laura's face and for a moment Laura was sure she was not going to respond. She was bracing herself for the blow when the other woman slowly raised her hand and offered it.

'How do you do, Miss Maclane?' she said politely, and Laura found she had to swallow a lump in her throat.

'Please, call me Laura,' she urged in a husky voice.

Maxine recovered her hand and rested it in her lap. 'Laura, then,' she agreed with a faint smile, and Laura was painfully aware that she had not been given the same leave. Maxine Harrington accepted her presence here, but her graciousness only went so far.

Her eyes were drawn to where Quinn stood behind Maxine's chair. He was regarding her quizzically, silently asking her what else she might have expected. Nobody wanted her here. She was on sufferance, nothing more. If he thought to dismay her, the effect was the opposite. She stiffened her spine, reminding herself she had always known it would be neither comfortable nor easy. A fact which was reinforced mere seconds later.

'Why have you come here?' Philip Harrington demanded aggressively. He was a younger copy of his father, and it caught at Laura's heart.

His mother winced. 'Philip, please. Things are quite bad enough without you making them worse,' she sighed.

'But it's what we all want to know, Mother. I think she wants to humiliate us all!'

Maxine sent her son a level look. 'If I am not humiliated, then there is no need for you to be. Laura is a guest in this house, and I expect you to treat her with courtesy.'

Laura knew how much it must have cost for her to say that, and she was impressed. Jonathan was right; Maxine Harrington had class.

'Thank you,' she responded gratefully. 'I hope that we can get better acquainted whilst I am here,' she added, and Maxine Harrington shot her a curious look.

'Perhaps,' she agreed distantly, then smiled coolly. 'I understand from Quinn that you run a business. I dare say you will not want to be away from it for long.'

It was delicately put, but Laura got the message loud and clear. She was not to outstay her welcome. She smiled wryly. 'No more than a few days,' she confirmed, putting a limit on her stay that the other woman could accept.

Maxine nodded. 'Then I hope you enjoy the holiday.'

'I'm sure I shall,' Laura replied with a smile, and the other woman relaxed back into her chair.

'It's unfortunate that you didn't tell us you were coming. I'm afraid you missed supper, but I'm sure Norah can find something for you.' She referred to the housekeeper.

Food was the last thing on Laura's mind. For all her outward poise, her stomach had been doing acrobatics ever since she had walked into the room. 'Thank you, but that won't be necessary. Jonathan and I ate before we started out.' She indicated the man standing just behind her.

Turning her attention to the familiar figure, Maxine

gave him a smile of such genuine warmth and welcome that Laura's heart twisted. She knew it was foolish to feel envious, but she couldn't help it. She wanted to be welcome here too.

'Jonathan, dear boy! I didn't see you there!' Maxine exclaimed, holding out her hands to him.

Jonathan offered Laura a supportive smile as he stepped past her. 'Maxine. How are you...?'

Laura looked on, wondering if she would ever be a part of this family. It occurred to her that they had no reason to accept her, ever. Even if, having heard the truth, they accepted it, they need not welcome her with open arms. She was nothing to them. They might always feel the way they did now. It was a sobering thought.

'Here. Take this.' Quinn suddenly appeared before her, and the husky-voiced command sent those by now familiar shivers down her spine.

She glanced from the cut glass full of golden liquid up into his face. Her eyes lingered on his disturbingly sensual lips. He really did have a beautiful mouth. She could envisage it seeking out tender skin, burning it with the intensity of his passion. It would be insistent, and... What in the world was she doing? Good God, was she insane? she groaned silently. She absolutely did not want to think those things about this abominable man!

'What's in it? Poison?' she quipped facetiously.

A hint of a smile curved his lips. 'I couldn't find any at such short notice. It's only brandy.'

She eyed him askance. 'Hmm. Do I believe you? You wouldn't care to taste it first?'

One eyebrow quirked at her. 'You could try trusting me,' he said, but sipped at the liquid all the same. 'Satisfied?' he asked softly, fixing her eyes with his as he held the glass out to her.

Her nerves gave a violent jolt. Surely she had imagined that that perfectly simple question had been laced with sexual connotations? Imagination or not, her senses were reacting in a way which had nothing to do with brandy and glasses, and everything to do with his closeness. She could smell him on every intake of breath. The spicy scent of his cologne tantalised her, whilst the heat of him seared her even though they did not touch. It made her aware of herself in a way she never had been before. Her senses were sharper, more perceptive. They made her want things that were downright dangerous. Like Quinn.

She was mad. Wanting Quinn Mannion was the height of insanity. He despised her, and she positively loathed him. Her brain knew it, so why didn't her senses follow suit?

She didn't know the answer, but suddenly she really needed that drink.

Inwardly she cursed the way her hand carried the faintest tremor as she reached out to take the glass. All would have been well even so, had not Quinn's fingers brushed against hers as she grasped it. Just like before, a tongue of flame went shooting up her arm. She gasped, her reaction instinctive. She jerked her hand away, and the glass wobbled precariously before tumbling to the carpet.

'Oh, no!' Laura exclaimed, watching the liquid run out. Fortunately the glass hadn't broken, but the contents were soaking in rapidly.

'I'll get a cloth,' Caroline declared with the practicality of a woman used to spills and the various other mishaps brought about by two lively youngsters.

Other reactions were predictably less constructive and more critical.

'It was her fault,' Stella accused, glaring at Laura. 'I saw it myself. You deliberately took your hand away just as Quinn was giving you that glass!'

Already unsettled by the accident, Laura lost her cool and took umbrage at that. 'Now just a minute—' she began, but Quinn interrupted her before she could get into a good flow.

'Don't be ridiculous, Stella,' he snapped impatiently. 'It was an accident. There's no need to make a federal case out of it,' he added shortly, and the younger woman bristled with affront.

'How can you possibly defend her?' she gasped, and Laura's eyes took on a dangerous glint.

'I don't need defending by anyone,' she pronounced firmly, and received a quelling look from the man at her side.

'Stay out of this, Laura,' Quinn ordered, and her lips tightened in annoyance. 'You've done quite enough for one evening,' he added tautly, and she drew in a furious breath. However, before she could utter a word, Caroline returned with various cloths, and Quinn pulled her out of the way.

To all intents and purposes they were now separated from the rest of the room. Uncomfortably aware of the sense of isolation, Laura folded her arms in front of her and glared at him balefully.

'What do you mean, I've done enough?'

'Trouble just naturally follows you around, doesn't it?' he jibed, setting her teeth on edge.

'What exactly are you accusing me of now?' she demanded to know.

'You have this unbelievable talent for picking fights with everyone in the room,' he denounced her, and she caught back her first sharp retort in favour of something more taunting. Her eyes glittered as her chin went up.

'Were you impressed?'

Those blue eyes sharpened intently. 'Did you expect me to be?'

Laura gave an offhand shrug. 'No, which was just as well, as I would have been disappointed. Not much impresses you, does it, Quinn?'

'I would be impressed by your sensitivity if you decided to leave,' he told her coolly, and she laughed in spite of herself. He was persistent.

'It appears we're both to be doomed to disappointment,' she sighed elaborately, watching Caroline climb to her feet. 'Will it be stained?' she asked in genuine concern.

Caroline brushed her hair from her forehead with the back of her hand, and puffed out a breath. 'It's hard to say. I suggest you have it professionally cleaned after the holiday, Maxine.'

'Naturally I shall get it done,' Laura insisted, for it was her fault the carpet was stained in the first place.

Across the room, Stella laughed scornfully. 'Oh really! You may have walked off with a chunk of the family fortune, but you can have no idea of the value of that carpet. You'll get Joe Smith to do it and ruin it!'

In her unsettled state, that was one insult too many for Laura. She counted to ten before losing her temper. 'You really shouldn't make those sort of value judgements, Stella. You don't have the brain power for it!' she returned caustically, drawing a collective breath from most of the adults in the room.

'Of all the nerve!' Philip exclaimed, shooting to his feet in defence of his sister.

'Mother, we cannot put up with this!' Stella cried at

the same time as Laura felt a strong hand close about her upper arm.

'I think you've said just about enough,' Quinn warned sibilantly.

'On the contrary, I'm just getting started,' she countered, trying to shake him off but failing miserably.

'Back off, before I get nasty,' he cautioned just loud enough for her to hear.

'Nasty? You're already breaking my arm,' she complained, turning her head and finding herself looking straight into his eyes. Her lips tightened at the mockery she found there. Her efforts amused him.

'Be thankful I'm not breaking your neck!' he retorted mildly, but his hold did ease a fraction, though not enough for her to escape.

'You are an obnoxious man!' she declared witheringly. All it did was make him grin.

'But too much of a gentleman to reply in kind.'

Laura knew that to struggle would be playing into his hands. Taking a deep breath, she sought the calm which always managed to get her through particularly taxing moments with difficult clients.

'Something tells me this might be a good moment to ask to be shown my room,' she observed wryly, and Quinn eyed her thoughtfully, clearly wondering what she was up to with this change of tack.

'That's the first sensible thing you've said all evening,' he agreed sardonically, and she longed to wipe the smile from his face.

'I happen to be an extremely intelligent woman,' she informed him loftily, and received a grunt of amusement for her pains.

'There's a hell of a difference between intelligence and cleverness. I'll admit you're clever, Laura Maclane, but that kind of cleverness relies on the stupidity of others.'

'You, of course, would never be that stupid?' she contested scathingly, and Quinn laughed.

'Not where you are concerned, anyway.'

It was the equivalent of waving a red rag at a bull. Laura couldn't resist retaliating. Licking her lips provocatively, she raised one perfectly arched eyebrow questioningly. 'You're that sure?' she taunted recklessly.

Quinn's eyes narrowed speculatively. 'Playing games can be dangerous, as I've told you before. Don't start something you'll regret.'

Laura laughed, though the warning sent a shiver of excitement down her spine. 'What makes you think I'm starting something? Poor Quinn, I do believe all those thrillers you write are beginning to make you paranoid. After all, who is holding whom?' she pointed out mockingly, glancing down to where his hand sat on her arm.

His hand didn't release her. Instead, it slipped down to her wrist and his thumb began a steady backwards and forwards movement over her pulse. 'I thought the point of the game was wanting me to touch you,' he drawled huskily, and Laura knew he could feel the way her heart was galloping.

Still, she was not ready to retreat. 'What game are you referring to?'

'The one where you come on to me so strongly, I forget all my principles and am overwhelmed by lust,' he enlarged for her benefit, bringing hot colour to her cheeks, though she tried to prevent it.

'Why on earth would I want you to do that?' she demanded witheringly, and drew a soft laugh from him.

'Because you're bored? Because it's been how many months, and you need a man? Because you want me?'

he added in a sexy undertone that rippled along her nerves, doing untold damage.

She went as still as a statue. 'What?'

'Don't tell me you didn't know?' Quinn goaded in amusement. 'Like me or loathe me, you want me.'

Shock tore through her at his stunning declaration. 'That is the most—' She hastened to deny it, but he didn't let her finish.

'I want you, too,' he confessed, taking her breath away. 'But before you get too excited it's only fair to warn you I have no intention of doing anything about it. Call me over-fastidious, but there are just some things I will not do. Top of the list is getting involved with someone who's gone round the block as often as you have.'

It was the very last thing she had expected him to say, and for a second she was too surprised to be insulted. Then it hit her, and anger surged up insider her. How dared he?

'My God, you've got a nerve!' she gasped furiously, but he merely laughed.

'Just how many men have you had?'

'Go to hell.'

'With you? I'll pass, thanks.'

Positively volcanic, Laura wanted to say so many things but not a word found its way from her mouth. Then, before she could take any other form of action, they were interrupted.

'Is everything all right over there?' Jonathan called out.

'We're fine,' Quinn put in before Laura could respond. 'Laura was saying she wanted to be shown her room. I was just about to take her upstairs.'

'That's kind of you, Quinn.' Maxine thanked him. 'The room next to yours is unoccupied. It's rather small,

I'm afraid,' she apologised to Laura, 'but as we had no idea you were coming all the other rooms have been taken.'

'Perhaps Laura expects to share Jonathan's room?' Philip put in snidely, and Laura, catching the look Jonathan sent Caroline and the dismayed expression on the other woman's face, would have gladly throttled him, half-brother or not.

'Thank you for the thought, Philip, but Jonathan is my friend and nothing more,' she said lightly, knowing that the best way to handle the remark was not to take it seriously. She let her gaze drift to Quinn's sister, and hoped she got the message. 'I will be perfectly satisfied with the room Maxine suggested, if Quinn will show me the way…?' She turned to find him regarding her curiously, but he was quick to respond to her suggestion.

'This way.'

Laura followed him back into the foyer and waited impatiently whilst he collected her case from where Jonathan had left it. They mounted the stairs side by side.

'That was a kind thing you did,' he remarked, and she didn't pretend not to know what he was referring to.

'Didn't you think I could be kind?' she said curtly.

'It never occurred to me.'

Now, why didn't that surprise her? 'But it did cross your mind to wonder if, since I came with Jonathan, I might be sleeping with him?' she countered dryly.

'It's been a long time between men, and you're not exactly the type of woman to respect other people's feelings. You take what you want. You could have taken Jonathan to your bed. My sister means nothing to you,' Quinn replied, and Laura smiled thinly. His opinion of her kept sinking lower and lower. Would it ever reach rock-bottom or was the well of his dislike bottomless?

'Believe it or not, I like your sister,' she said honestly.

They reached the landing and turned right.

Quinn cast her a sidelong look. 'You hardly know her. You've scarcely exchanged a dozen words.' Arriving at a door at the end of the hall, he threw it open and reached in to flick on the light.

Laura stepped inside and cast an appreciative glance around her. The room wasn't large, but it was comfortably furnished and decorated in autumn colours. 'Jonathan loves her, and that's good enough for me,' she enlarged, facing him again.

Quinn walked past her and deposited her case on the bed. 'Caroline is only just beginning to realise she loves him, too. I didn't expect you to notice it.'

'Or care if I did!'

'Or care,' he conceded with a nod, slipping his hands into his trouser pockets and regarding her steadily. 'Do you expect an apology?''

He was so blatant in his judgement, she had to laugh. 'I wouldn't hold my breath.'

Quinn nodded and smiled to himself, then took her completely by surprise by closing the space between them in two swift strides. One long-fingered hand reached out to cup her chin. Startled, she froze as his thumb began a slow caress along her jaw. Her eyes widened as danger signals went off in her head, urging her to move. But he had outmanoeuvred her and, though she did lift a hand, instead of brushing his hand away her fingers closed about his wrist and held on as a delicious, tingling warmth began to expand from the spot. Her brain seemed to grow sluggish, and her eyelids grew so heavy it took all her energy to stop them from closing. They fluttered.

Quinn laughed softly, and her eyes shot to his. 'You're very good,' he said quietly, and it took a second or two for his meaning to sink in.

He believed her reaction had been part of the games she played. He believed women like her used their attraction to the opposite sex to lure them into their trap. Which, whilst it was not true, at least hid the fact that she had been totally caught up in the moment. That piece of information she would keep from him at all costs.

Discovering a talent for acting she had previously been unaware of, Laura pulled away, flouncing out of his reach. 'If you aren't going to buy, don't touch the merchandise!' she protested, which had the desired effect of making his eyes narrow.

'Just what value do you put on yourself?' he asked coldly, and she smiled.

'More than you can afford, darling.'

Now it was his turn to smile, albeit grimly. 'Oh, I could buy you ten times over if I wanted. Alex's fortune was peanuts compared to mine. Doesn't it stick in your craw to know that I'm one man you will never have?'

Laura crossed her arms, allowing a tiny smile to curve the corners of her mouth. 'Never is an awfully long time. How can you be so sure?'

'Because I only play by my rules, and I always win.'

'You could lose this time.'

'I think not. You're no match for me, Laura Maclane. So, are we beginning to understand each other?'

'Oh, I think I'm beginning to understand you very well, Quinn, darling,' she drawled sardonically, and he smiled as he headed for the door.

'We'll see, Laura, darling,' he said as he went out and closed the door after him.

Grabbing up a pillow, she flung it at the door. She was so furious, it made her want to spit. She wasn't surprised to find she was shaking. The arrogance of the man, she fumed, pacing angrily across the floor and back again. What had he said? He wanted her but he wasn't going to act upon it with someone who had been around the block as often as she had? Of all the nerve!

She would just see about that! She would make Quinn Mannion eat his words if it was the last thing she did. He was so sure of himself. So certain that he would never lose control. Hah! She was going to prove him wrong. She would have him on his knees, begging her to make love to him!

Calming a little, she chewed her lip. Of course, she would have to be careful. There would be no point in building a trap and then getting caught in it herself. It wouldn't be easy, because he had proved to her that he could affect her strongly with a mere touch. But she was forewarned now. She could handle it.

A smile slowly spread across her face. Before she left this house again, she would make him regret he had ever met her. Just see if she didn't!

CHAPTER THREE

BY THE following morning Laura's anger had abated somewhat, but she was still of the same mind. She was determined to teach Quinn a lesson he would not forget in a hurry. In the back of her mind she knew she was acting out of character, but the knowledge wasn't strong enough to sway her.

A glance out of the window when she woke up had shown her that yesterday's dusting of snow had been hardened by an overnight frost, and she had dressed accordingly. Now she studied her reflection in the dressing-table mirror, and nodded with satisfaction. She knew she looked good in her tartan trousers and pink lambswool sweater. Good enough for Quinn to give her a second look, she hoped.

A shiver of anticipation ran down her spine. She had never actively gone out of her way to seduce a man before and, to be honest, she didn't know if she could. How hard could it be? Obviously it would help if the man were willing to be seduced, which didn't describe Quinn. However, she was not going to be faint-hearted, for she had a point to prove.

Leaving her room, she was heading for the stairs when she saw Caroline come out of a room ahead of her. The other woman hesitated when she saw Laura then, with a visible squaring of her shoulders, waited, giving Laura the distinct impression that she had something on her mind.

Intrigued, Laura quickened her step. 'Good morning,'

49

she greeted with a friendly smile. As she had told Quinn last night, she liked his sister, and hoped to make a friend of her. After all, she wasn't responsible for the kind of man her brother was.

'Good morning,' Caroline responded with more reserve, clearly uncertain of the best way to respond to Laura's friendliness. 'Did you sleep well?'

'Like a top,' Laura acknowledged, falling into step as they went on their way.

'Really? I thought you might have trouble sleeping,' Caroline remarked casually, and Laura looked at her quizzically.

'Because of my conscience, you mean?' she teased, and could have kicked herself when the other woman flushed. Instantly she laid a hand on her arm, bringing her to a halt. 'Forgive me. That was a crass thing to say.'

Caroline gave her a long, hard look, then shook her head in confusion. 'You're not at all how I imagined you to be.'

Laura shrugged. 'What can I say? I flunked Bitchiness 101. Nobody's perfect,' she proclaimed deprecatingly, and was pleased to hear Caroline giggle.

'That's what I mean. The woman I expected wouldn't say thing's like that. I like you, and I never expected to.'

'In that case, it will be easier for you to ask me whatever it is that's bothering you, won't it?' Laura encouraged with another smile, taking her companion aback.

'How did you…? No, don't answer that. Quinn always tells me my face is an open book,' Caroline declared wryly, then searched Laura's face for several seconds before coming to a decision. 'You're right, I do have something to ask,' she confessed.

'We could go somewhere private if you want,' Laura suggested, trying to put her at ease, but Caroline quickly shook her head.

'No, no, this is fine. I just... Oh, darn it! Did you mean what you said about Jon last night?' she finally blurted out, and Laura suddenly realised why Caroline was so ill at ease. She expected to hear the worst.

'Every word,' she confirmed readily. 'Jonathan has only ever been a friend.'

'I see,' Caroline said slowly, embarrassed colour washing into her cheeks. 'You must think I've very foolish,' she sighed.

'Not in the least,' Laura hastened to assure her.

Caroline clearly felt the need to explain. 'I loved my husband very much, you know. I never thought I would find someone else, and especially not that it would turn out to be Jon. After my husband died, Jon was always there to help. I used to call him my rock, and relied on him tremendously. I don't know when I started seeing him differently. I didn't know I could be jealous, until last night,' she added with a wry smile. 'I thought... Well, you know what I thought.'

Laura pulled a face. 'I imagine you wanted to scratch my eyes out.'

'Something like that,' Caroline agreed with a laugh. 'I'm sorry.'

Laura waved that away. 'There's no need to be. I'm glad we've sorted it out. You see, I happen to think you and Jonathan will make an ideal couple, and I wouldn't want to come between you.'

The other woman shook her head in bewilderment. 'You know, you're really very nice.'

'For a woman who snaffled a fortune out from under

the noses of the Harrington family,' Laura pointed out ironically.

Caroline sent her a curious look. 'I can't say I wasn't shocked, but Alex was entitled to leave his money where he wanted. If he chose to leave some of it to you, I'm sure he had his reasons.'

Laura glanced down, studying her nails. 'Most newspapers would suggest Alexander was incapable of rational thought because I used my body to addle his brains.'

'And what do you say to that?' Caroline countered curiously.

'I say let them think what they like. It doesn't bother me,' Laura declared indifferently, and Caroline laughed scoffingly.

'I just saw my first flying pig,' she said good-humouredly. 'Believe me, with two inventive children, I know a lie when I hear it. It does bother you. In fact, I would go so far as to say it hurts you,' she said gently, and, after staring at her for a moment, Laura had to look away, sudden emotion clogging her throat.

'I cared for him,' she said huskily. 'Very much.'

Caroline frowned. 'I can see that. This is so confusing. I feel I'm missing something.'

Alarm bells sounded, and Laura hastily cleared her throat. 'According to your brother, like you, I'm an open book,' she remarked, hoping to steer the other woman away from dangerous ground.

'Oh, him!' Caroline dismissed Quinn with a wave of her hand. 'He's a man. What does he know?'

Laura grinned at this display of sisterly affection. 'I bet you don't let him hear you say things like that.'

Caroline grinned back. 'You'd be right, too.' From down below a clock chimed, and her eyes widened. 'Is that the time? You'd better get down before all the food goes.'

They carried on towards the stairs, and it was when they were halfway down that Caroline passed a remark which stopped Laura in her tracks.

'I've been wondering. Have we ever met before? You look kind of familiar.'

'Do I? I don't believe we've met. I'm sure I would remember,' Laura replied, doing her best to sound unconcerned, whilst recalling that Alexander had told her she had his eyes. Was that what Caroline had noticed? If so, how long would it be before the others saw it too? Perhaps that would solve her problem. On the other hand, it might make it even more complicated.

The other woman smiled vaguely. 'Mmm, I'm sure you're right. Oh, well, I'd better find out what my dear children are doing. I left them in Quinn's care, but he's a pushover!'

Laura couldn't quite see Quinn in that light, but then, she wasn't his sister.

Caroline led the way into an already crowded breakfast room, and Laura cast a look around the table. Only Stella was missing. Quinn sat with his back to her, and her eyes were drawn to the breadth of his shoulders beneath his sweater. She was willing to bet there wasn't a spare ounce of flesh on him. He would be tanned and firm to the touch, and... She had better get hold of her thoughts before they could trespass onto more dangerous ground. She was supposed to be turning him on, not herself.

Jonathan was deep in conversation with Maxine, but he forgot what he was saying when Caroline entered the room. When he saw the two of them together, his brows rose, and behind Caroline's back Laura grinned broadly and made an 'OK' sign with her fingers.

As Caroline went to sit beside him, Laura became aware that Quinn had turned round in his chair and was watching her broodingly. When her eyes met his, the expression in them kept her rooted to the spot. It was bold, and quite stunningly electric. Her nerves rioted, and all at once there might have been only the two of them in the room. Awareness leapt between them like a living, breathing entity. It stole the breath from her lungs and set hot blood pulsing through her veins. His eyes dropped to her mouth, and her lips tingled as if he had actually touched them. They parted on a soft sigh. Suddenly she longed for him to kiss her. She desperately wanted to know what his mouth would feel like. How hot it would be; how it would taste. And, looking into his eyes, she saw the same desire there. It was shocking. It was unutterably exciting.

Until she saw his lip curl, and cold amusement fill those previously hot blue orbs. Now they repeated the message of last night. They told her they knew she liked what she saw, as did he, but that there was no way on God's good earth that he would ever do anything to satisfy that need.

It was like a douche of cold water, and brought her back to her senses with a wallop. She knew he believed he had just led her into thinking she had a chance with him, at which point he had calculatingly pulled the rug out from under her feet. Oh, he had been devastating, all right, but it only served to remind her of her intention to make him eat his words. Because he wanted her. He had made no attempt to conceal it. It was a weapon she could use against him and consequently, instead of being cowed, she came back with all guns blazing.

Her eyes flashed back their own message: I'm going to change your mind.

His amusement deepened. Better women than you have tried, and failed, his eyes taunted right back.

How long this silent exchange might have gone on it was impossible to say, for just then Ellie giggled, breaking the spell which held them, and the sounds of the room returned. Laura watched Quinn turn back to the table and smiled tightly. If he thought she was giving up, he was mistaken. There were chinks in his armour, and while the iron was hot she would strike with it.

As she approached the table, her path took her close to where Quinn sat, and as she passed him her hand ran a light caress over his shoulder, her fingers brushing against the nape of his neck. She felt his start of surprise at her touch, and her lips curved in satisfaction even as she noted that her fingertips tingled from the brief contact.

'Good morning, Quinn, darling,' she breathed just loud enough for him to hear as she took the only other empty chair, which just happened to be beside him.

Quinn eyed her consideringly as she accepted the cup of coffee which Norah, the housekeeper, placed before her. She tipped her head to one side, eyebrows lifting ingenuously, silently asking if anything was wrong. Those eyes took on a spine-tingling gleam.

'You look well rested,' he observed smoothly, and she nodded.

'I slept dreamlessly. Now I'm ready for anything,' she added provokingly, and held her breath for Quinn's response.

Unfortunately, Philip, who was unashamedly listening in to their conversation, interrupted before Quinn could speak. 'Of course she slept well; she doesn't have a conscience to bother her,' he sneered, and Laura sighed heavily. She had been hoping to avoid confrontation.

Aware that she was suddenly the centre of attention, she chose her words carefully. 'Please, Philip, I don't want to argue with you. All I want to do is have breakfast in peace,' she said pacifically, hoping to head him off, but the young man was determined.

'It's disgusting having to sit here with the cheap little tart who tricked my father out of his money!' he cried out viciously, taking the colour from her cheeks.

'Philip, no!' his mother protested, ashen-faced.

Laura met eyes that were stormy with anger and grief. The knowledge closed her throat. He was lashing out at her because she was there, and he was a young man in pain. She could understand that. She missed their father, too.

'I miss Alexander as much as you do,' she forced out, but her half-brother didn't want to hear that. He shot to his feet as if propelled from a gun.

'How could you? He wasn't your father!'

Though he didn't know it, he had dealt her a body blow. She wanted to cry out that Alexander was her father, but could not. Stricken, her eyes sought Jonathan's and found sympathy there. 'Nevertheless, I know how it feels to lose someone you love.'

Philip's jaw worked madly, and he was perilously close to tears. 'I don't want your sympathy! You're nobody! I hate you!'

Laura felt the sting of her own suppressed tears, and hastily pushed her cup away. She could not afford to break down before all these people. 'I think I'll just go outside for a while,' she declared uncomfortably.

She was about to stand up when a strong hand closed over hers and compelled her to stay where she was. She looked at Quinn in surprise, but his gaze was firmly fixed on the young man who stood trembling with anger across the table.

'Stay where you are, Laura. If anyone leaves, it should be Philip. But not before he has apologised,' he said sternly.

Laura looked from one to the other. 'That isn't necessary,' she insisted, wanting only to leave and lick her wounds. Quinn was making things worse. Philip would never forgive her for his humiliation.

'Quinn is absolutely right,' Maxine affirmed, shocking her son and Laura alike.

Philip's eyes looked ready to pop out. 'Mother!'

'I'm sorry if this hurts you, Philip, but this is my house and I won't tolerate such behaviour, even from you,' she informed her son. 'Laura is a guest, and you'll apologise to her.'

The young man looked as if he wanted to kill somebody, Laura by preference. 'I'm not a child, and I will not apologise. If you want to cosy up with her, go ahead, but I'm leaving. Come on, Alison,' he urged his girlfriend, who, with a nervous smile which encompassed everyone, followed him out of the room.

Silence followed his departure, and Laura felt the weight of guilt on her shoulders. 'I'm sorry, Mrs Harrington. That was my fault,' she apologised, but the other woman shook her head.

'It's kind of you to say so, but it's not true. Philip created the scene, not you. He is still most upset by the death of his father. He's a sensitive boy.'

Which left Laura with the unhappy knowledge that, had she not been present, the whole thing would never have happened. It was her presence in the house which was causing all the undercurrents. A quick glance at

Quinn told her that the point was not lost on him. Although he had defended her, he blamed her, and she knew he was right to do so.

The older woman folded her napkin with shaking hands and rose stiffly to her feet. 'Excuse me. I think I had better go and speak to my son.' Gathering her dignity about her, she left the room, closing the door quietly after her.

'Well, you certainly know how to clear a room,' Quinn declared mordantly into the awkward silence which followed her exit.

Caroline's gentle voice intervened. 'Tom, if you've had enough to eat, why don't you take Ellie and go play outside?' she suggested calmly, as if nothing out of the ordinary had happened.

Tom, precocious and without fear, looked interestedly at all the adults. 'Is Laura going to fight with Uncle Quinn again?' he asked cheerfully, as if it was to be considered a treat. His mother rolled her eyes, but at least it had the effect of breaking the tension as everyone laughed.

Laura silently blessed him, for he had restored her equilibrium. She hadn't expected to be so vulnerable to the feelings of her half-brother and sister. She would have to develop a thicker skin, or she would soon be an emotional wreck.

'No, we're not going to fight, Tom,' Quinn informed his nephew, trying to sound stern but failing dismally.

'See, we're holding hands,' Laura added, giving Quinn a sidelong look. He immediately made to remove his hand, but she was too quick for him. In the blink of an eye, she had turned her hand and captured his, holding on tight. After that first attempt, he surprised her by seeming to be quite happy to leave his hand where it was.

In fact, he chose to back her up. 'People don't fight when they're holding hands, do they?'

'Nah, they do all that kissing stuff,' Tom remarked disgustedly, whilst his sister's eyes widened.

'Is Uncle Quinn going to kiss the witch lady, Mama?' Ellie asked in awe, and Laura choked back a laugh at the look on her expressive little face.

'Not unless he wants to get turned into a frog,' Jonathan teased, reaching out to ruffle her hair.

'Thank you very much. You're a big help,' Caroline declared exasperatedly, turning to her offspring with as much sternness as she could muster. 'Listen up. Nobody is going to fight, and nobody is going to kiss anyone else. And she is not the witch lady, Ellie. You must call her Laura, OK?'

'OK, Mama,' Ellie murmured obediently, but she gave Laura and Quinn a look which said she still wasn't sure.

'Off you go, then,' Caroline urged, and Tom was down from the table like a shot, heading out of the room with his sister at his heels. Caroline rolled her eyes and rose too. 'Oh, well, no peace for the wicked. I'll have to go and make sure they're dressed warmly. Excuse me.'

As she left, Ian Nevin, who had sat through the entire proceedings in silence, folded up the newspaper he had been reading and tucked it under his arm. The look he sent Laura was wryly amused. 'Thank you for an interesting half-hour. I've no doubt we'll be doing it again soon. I'm off to see how Stella is doing.'

'Take her some tea and biscuits. Caroline swore by it,' Quinn suggested, and Ian nodded his thanks before disappearing into the kitchen.

Jonathan looked questioningly at Quinn. 'Is Stella pregnant?'

Quinn nodded, not bothering to disguise his amusement. 'Just barely, and she's not having a good time of it.'

'I thought she didn't want children,' Jonathan remarked as Laura tried to picture the scornful young woman with children of her own.

Strangely enough, it didn't prove difficult at all. She could imagine her half-sister handling messy diapers with no trouble. Just like her brother, Stella was angry and grieving, but she had to contend with the early stages of pregnancy too. Her hormones must be a mess. Laura could imagine the mood swings she was going through, and her ready sympathy was aroused.

'Apparently Ian changed her mind,' Quinn was saying when she tuned back in to the conversation, and Jonathan laughed.

'I'll be damned. Stella with a baby. The mind boggles. Will she know which end is up?'

'Don't be cruel!' Laura interposed swiftly. 'Stella will make a perfectly fine mother.'

Quinn's brows rose. 'You're supporting her? Since when did she become your friend?'

Since I discovered she was my half-sister, Laura was tempted to say, but didn't. 'It's a woman thing,' she explained airily, just as a telephone rang nearby. A few seconds later the housekeeper poked her head round the kitchen door.

'It's for you, Mr Jonathan.'

Frowning, he stood up. 'I don't know who that can be. I'll take it in the study, thanks, Norah. Sorry about this.'

Laura watched him leave and turned to look at Quinn.

'Alone at last,' she quipped, and wasn't quite prepared for the sultry look he turned on her. Her heart kicked as he glanced down at their still linked hands and slowly ran his thumb over her fingers before extracting his hand.

'Didn't your parents ever tell you it was dangerous to play with fire?' he asked in his faintly husky voice and, despite the overlying distaste, Laura felt the sound all the way to her toes. It was amazingly hard to respond with a jaunty retort, yet she managed it.

'Oh, yes,' she confirmed brightly, reaching for her coffee and sipping at the cooling liquid. 'However, when I grew up I discovered that forbidden things are much more fun,' she flirted daringly, watching over the edge of the cup for his reaction. He didn't disappoint her.

Sitting sideways on his chair, he stretched out his long legs and eyed her speculatively. 'As a matter of interest, do you draw the line at anything?'

She pretended to give it some thought, then shook her head. 'Not so far. I'm pretty broad-minded.'

'You would have to be, to take a fifty-one-year-old man as your lover.'

It was a comment calculated to make her hackles rise for there was no room in it, or his mind, for doubt. It never occurred to him he might be wrong. Well, she was not going to be the one to put him straight. He expected a money-hungry temptress, and he was going to get one.

Hoping that, wherever he was, her father would understand and forgive her deception, Laura set her cup down, rested her chin on her hand and curved her lips into a cat-like smile. 'Alexander was young for his age. We were perfectly compatible,' she added, deliberately moving her other hand until it rested on Quinn's forearm. 'Though I imagine we'd be better.'

Quinn's lips curved. 'You do, do you? Why is that?'

Laura watched her fingers trace the pattern on his sleeve, then raised her eyes to his. 'Because you have more imagination,' she said softly, alluringly, allowing the very tip of her tongue to peep out and moisten her lips. She had never dared do anything quite so suggestive to a man before, and her heart began to gallop madly.

Now Quinn allowed himself a smile, but it was so chilling in its brilliance that it sent a shiver down her spine. 'You don't listen too well, do you? Let me tell you again. What you are trying to do isn't going to work.'

Undaunted, her voice took on a huskiness of its own. 'Maybe I'm not trying to do anything,' she denied.

'And maybe the moon is made of green cheese,' he responded sardonically.

'Why would I lie?'

'Possibly because you and the truth have only a passing acquaintance. To people like you, the truth is whatever is convenient at the time.'

'People like me?' she queried, tempted to dig her nails into his arm until they drew blood. Arrogant man!

Quinn let his gaze wander over the delicate bones of her face before he answered. 'Women with an eye on the main chance. I should imagine the absolute truth would be inappropriate,' he enlarged as his eyes found her lips.

To her chagrin, they tingled as if he had actually touched them and Laura had to stifle a groan at this example of his lethal charm. 'Have you never told a white lie?' she asked with a revealing hint of breathlessness.

If he heard it, he gave no sign. 'For what purpose?'

'To get your way with a woman.'

'Ah.'

So, he was a proponent of the double standard, was he? A mocking smile tweaked her lips. 'That's different, is it?'

Quinn's eyes met and held hers. 'I never took a single one of them for their money,' he said levelly.

She winced inwardly. Ouch. He had neatly turned the tables on her and all she could do for now was let him go and sit back in her seat with a large sigh, conceding him that round.

'*Touché.*'

Quinn's expression grew thoughtful. 'You're not going to deny it?'

Laura picked up her cup of now cold coffee and sipped at it. 'How can I? The money is mine, and everyone knows it.' She shrugged carelessly.

'What are you going to do with it? Go on a spending spree?'

She eyed him quizzically. Trust him to think that. 'I might surprise you.'

He laughed. 'I doubt very much that you'd give it away to worthy causes. Your kind think charity begins at home. You must find yourself in urgent need of a new dress, or a diamond necklace.'

Laura set her cup down carefully. He was beginning seriously to annoy her with this 'your kind' talk. 'What makes you think Alexander hasn't given me all that already?' she challenged, and had the satisfaction of seeing his beautiful mouth twist in distaste.

'I was forgetting,' he said derisively. 'Alex probably spent a small fortune on you before he died.'

If her cup had been a blunt instrument, she would dearly have loved to sock him over the head with it.

Hiding her anger, she smiled reminiscently, knowing it would annoy him.

'He was very generous,' she said softly, thinking not of the statement she was backing up but of the long conversations they had had. He had been generous with the things she considered important. His time and his affection.

'And you milked him for all he was worth.'

He was so scornful it made her laugh. 'I would have taken more if I could,' she averred unrepentantly. She would always regret that she could not have known him longer.

Quinn's eyes registered his disgust. 'Ain't that the truth?'

Before Laura could respond to that, the door opened and Jonathan came back into the room.

'Sorry,' he apologised as he resumed his seat. Glancing from one to the other, he sighed knowingly. 'Well, at least there's no blood and you're both still alive,' he observed drolly.

'Barely,' Quinn retorted, getting up.

'Going somewhere?' Laura asked sweetly, finding her eyes drawn to the way Quinn's jeans hugged his legs, showing off their muscular length in a way which dried her mouth.

'A little of your company goes a long way, Laura, darling. I'm going to take myself out for a breath of fresh air to prepare myself for round two.'

'I'll look forward to it.'

At the door, he halted long enough to send her a cautionary look. 'I wouldn't get my hopes up if I were you.'

'No more than they need be. I intend to win on points.'

'Whilst I, sweetheart, intend nothing less than a

knockout!' he rejoined, and closed the door firmly behind him.

'What was that all about?' Jonathan demanded uneasily, and Laura grimaced. One thing she did know; Jonathan would not approve of what she was doing.

'You don't want to know,' she warned.

'I know I don't, but you'd better tell me anyway,' he said in his no-nonsense, courtroom voice.

Laura shook her head. 'It's private. A game. Between Quinn and me.'

He frowned. 'It sounds like a damned dangerous game to me!'

'It is,' she agreed with a faint smile. 'But I intend to win it.'

'Why does that leave me less than reassured?' he groaned as she rose and came towards him. Bending over, she dropped a kiss on the top of his head.

'Because you're a good friend and you worry about me. Believe me, you don't have to. Trust me on this,' she urged, then, with a pat on his shoulder, left the room.

Jonathan stared after her helplessly. It had been his experience that when someone said 'trust me', that was the moment when he should do the exact opposite!

CHAPTER FOUR

LAURA didn't see Quinn again until later that afternoon. He hadn't put in an appearance at lunch, although Philip was present, subdued and silent. Laura felt sorry for him, but she knew he would bitterly resent anything she said. All in all, she was not making the kind of impression she wanted with her family.

After lunch everyone seemed to disappear about their own business and, left to fend for herself, Laura made herself comfortable in the lounge with a magazine. Not that she read much of it. Her thoughts kept drifting to Quinn. She couldn't help wondering what he was doing—and who he was doing it with. When she realised what she was doing, she got annoyed with herself and tossed the glossy aside. Whatever he was doing, it was no business of hers.

'Oh!'

The soft exclamation drew Laura's head round. Stella hovered in the doorway.

'Excuse me,' she muttered, turning to go, and Laura hastily clambered to her feet.

'Don't go,' she said swiftly then, as Stella looked at her in surprise, gave a tiny, helpless shrug. 'I mean, don't let me drive you away.'

Stella thought for a bit, then slowly walked into the room. 'You couldn't,' she returned coldly, and Laura grimaced. Her half-sister was not about to make this easy.

'Are you feeling better now?' she asked, watching

Stella choose a chair some way away from her and sit down. Laura sat too.

'Yes, thank you,' the younger woman answered shortly, watching Laura with cool grey eyes.

Laura took a deep breath. Trying to make conversation was like wading through quicksand. 'You must be looking forward to the baby.'

With the first natural gesture Laura had seen her make, Stella rested her hand on her tummy. 'Very much, though I don't know what kind of mother I shall make,' she responded honestly.

'I'm sure you'll be very good at it,' Laura told her, smiling, but received a long, cold look for her pains.

'Don't patronise me.'

Colour stained Laura's cheeks. 'I can assure you I was doing no such thing, Stella.'

The young woman shrugged indifferently. 'Whatever.'

Laura found her temper shortening dramatically and it took quite an effort to keep from saying something impetuous, like 'Grow up'. 'I would like to be your friend, you know,' she said instead, and received an incredulous look.

'I can't imagine why!' Stella returned and, hearing it, Laura found herself agreeing with her. Why on earth was she bothering?

'I give up!' she exclaimed in defeat, and could have smacked her half-sister when she smiled.

'Is that all, then? Can I go now?' Stella asked insolently, and didn't wait for an answer before getting up and leaving the room.

'Please yourself,' Laura muttered after her departing back, feeling depressed. She was certain both Philip and Stella could be nice people under different circumstances, but they were being downright obnoxious now. Not that she could blame them. They had no idea who she was, and her connection with their father hardly put her in a favourable light. She just wished they would bend a little. Give her some hope and encouragement.

Which was wishful thinking of the worst kind. Deciding she must do something other than sit there feeling sorry for herself, Laura got up again and strode from the room. She was on her way to the stairs when Caroline came down them with Tom and Ellie. One look at her face was enough to tell Laura all was not well.

'What's wrong?' she asked in concern, studying the other woman's chalk-white face.

'It's just a migraine,' Caroline excused, but Laura, who suffered from them occasionally herself, knew it was far from 'just' anything.

'I think you should go right to bed and sleep it off,' Laura suggested, but Caroline shook her head.

'I can't. I promised to take the children for a walk to the lake.'

Laura looked down at the two urchins who hovered at their mother's side. She gave them a bright smile which Tom answered with a grin. She wanted to help, but she doubted they would go off with her. Which was wise for their safety but hardly helped now. As luck would have it, at that very moment Jonathan appeared from the back of the house, giving her an answer to the problem.

'Don't worry about Tom and Ellie. Jonathan and I will take them,' she declared, looking expectantly at her friend.

He did not disappoint her. Quick to size up the situation, he spared Caroline one all-encompassing glance before speaking to her children. 'How about it, kids? Do

you want to come with Laura and me? Give your mom
a chance to get better?'

'OK,' Tom agreed quickly, but Ellie took a little
longer. Finally she took a step away from her mother
and tucked her tiny hand in Jonathan's.

Laura saw him take a decidedly shaky breath, and
knew it was a very significant moment for him. He loved
Caroline, and he loved her children too. He desperately
wanted them to accept him. It seemed now that they had.

'You go on up,' she told a relieved Caroline. 'We'll
make sure they wrap up warmly.'

Feeling too ill to argue, Caroline still spared a moment
to catch her son's attention. 'Just you make sure you
behave yourself,' she admonished him before taking herself up to her room.

There followed ten minutes of miniature mayhem as
they all changed into warmer clothes. Although the sun
was shining, there was no real warmth to the day. Once
they got into the shade, it would be quite chilly. The last
thing anyone needed was a cold on Christmas Day.

'Is Uncle Quinn coming too?' Ellie asked when they
were once more downstairs, and Laura was helping her
into her padded coat.

Squatting down in front of her, Laura held out one
woollen glove for the little girl to put her hand in. 'I
shouldn't think so.'

'Why not?' Ellie wanted to know, raising her chin so
that Laura could fix her scarf.

Laura sat back on her heels. 'Well, I don't suppose
anyone thought to ask him.'

'Can I ask him?'

Laura had to smile at the pleading look on the little
face. 'Honey, I don't know where your uncle Quinn is,'
she pointed out regretfully.

Ellie's face lit up. 'I do. He's right there!' she declared, pointing over Laura's shoulder, and as Laura twisted round to look Quinn walked in through the front door.

It seemed like magic, but she realised the little girl must have seen him through the window. What was magic was the tingle that went through her at the sight of him. In jeans and black leather jacket, with wind-blown hair and pink cheeks, he looked stunningly attractive.

'Uncle Quinn!' Ellie squealed, running over to him and throwing her arms around his legs—the only part of him she could reach.

Laughing, Quinn bent down and swung her up into his arms. 'Hi, short stuff. Where are you off to?' he asked his niece, but over her shoulder his eyes watched Laura as she stood up.

His blue gaze ranged over her trim figure, and her body responded to that all-encompassing look. Her nipples hardened, pushing against the woollen fabric of her sweater with a swiftness and sensitivity which didn't surprise her. Her reaction to this man had always been strong and immediate. She was glad she had changed into jeans and a warmer, chunkier sweater, though, because it hid her more revealing reaction from him.

'Mama's sick, and we're going to the lake. Are you coming with us?' Ellie's treble cut through the invisible cord which spanned the air between them.

'Sick?' He frowned, seeking clarity from Laura.

'A migraine,' she enlarged just before one small hand urged Quinn's head round.

'Uncle Quinn! Are you coming?'

Quinn struggled with a grin. 'Wouldn't miss it for the

world. Do you have any objection to me joining the party?' he asked as he turned to Laura.

Laura took her coat from the closet and slipped it on, pulling a pair of gloves from one of the pockets. It would be more comfortable without him, but she knew she didn't have the right to refuse to allow him to join them.

'None at all. A walk will do us all good. Of course, if you're too cold and tired to go out again...' she goaded with a shrug as Quinn set Ellie back on her feet.

'Doubting my stamina, Laura? Or my strength of will?' he enquired lightly. 'For your information, both are in perfect working order.'

'What's in perfect working order?' Jonathan asked as he and Tom came to join them. They had had to go upstairs in search of Tom's missing gloves.

Blue eyes locked with grey. 'Oh, just my ability to withstand the worst the fates can throw at me,' Quinn drawled sardonically. 'Come on, let's get going before I change my mind,' he rallied, leading the way outside.

The house was several miles from the nearest town, surrounded by hills and woodland. Most of the trees were bare now, but Laura was sure it would look beautiful in summer. They followed a well-used track into the trees, Tom and Ellie running on ahead. Although the temperature had risen a degree or two, here in the woods the ground was still hard with frost, making the footing treacherous in places.

Laura slipped once, and it was only Quinn's quick thinking which prevented her from hitting the ground hard. He scooped her up against him, and she wasn't sure if the sudden acceleration of her heart was due to the near accident or being held so close to his firm body. She suspected it was the latter, and quickly pushed herself upright before she could do something silly like press herself closer.

'Thank you,' she said stiffly, and he grunted.

'Next time you try that, I'll let you fall,' he responded tersely, and her eyes darted to his in surprise.

'What?' she gasped in disbelief.

'You heard me. Don't try it again.'

Her hand shot out, stopping him in his tracks. 'Hold on a minute. That was an accident,' she protested, and he sent her a knowing look.

'Sure it was. And you're as innocent as the day is long,' he jeered, setting her teeth on edge.

Laura shook her head. 'My God, you have a suspicious mind,' she declared as she turned on her heel and hurried after Jonathan and the children.

'You'd do well to remember it,' he called after her, but she ignored him. Only a fool would risk serious injury by pretending to fall in these conditions. He ought to know that. As far as she was concerned, that was taking the need to dislike her too far.

Twenty minutes after they had started out, they emerged from the trees onto the banks of a small lake which had completely frozen over. Laura sat down on a large boulder and watched the children wander to the water's edge and begin skating stones over the ice.

Quinn propped one foot on the rock beside her and scanned the area carefully.

'Are you sure you want to stand this close to me?' she asked him dryly, and he glanced down at her speculatively. 'I could be about to fling myself off this rock.'

'I doubt you'll make the same mistake twice,' he told her mockingly, returning his attention to the skyline.

'What are you looking for?' Laura asked curiously after trying to see what was absorbing him, and failing.

'Sometimes you can see a hawk here.'

'Really?' She sat up straighter, squinting into the distance in the hopes of catching sight of one. 'Are they easy to spot?'

'When you know what you're looking for. At this time of year, food is scarcer. You most often see them circling, looking for prey.'

'I had no idea you were interested in birds,' she remarked, and he turned his head to give her a mocking smile.

'That's because you really know very little about me.'

'I know more than you think. Alexander used to speak of you often,' she countered.

One eyebrow lifted. 'Really? I'm surprised you found the time to talk,' he returned sardonically.

Her teeth came together with a snap. Positively fuming, Laura glared at him. 'You are the most loathsome man!' she spluttered, and Jonathan laid a calming hand on her arm.

'Take it easy, Laura,' he cautioned. 'Quinn's just trying to get a rise out of you.'

'Is that what I'm doing?' Quinn mocked, looking thoughtfully from one to the other.

'Hey, what are those two up to?' Jonathan exclaimed, and they both turned to see the two children trotting along the shoreline away from them. 'I'll go get them,' he said, and set off after them, his long legs eating up the distance.

'He's very protective of you,' Quinn remarked idly, and Laura tensed. It was her experience that Quinn didn't make idle comments.

'He's a good friend,' she admitted, but Quinn shook his head.

'No, it's more than that,' he mused, frowning, setting

her heart racing in sudden alarm. 'What is it about you that makes apparently intelligent men forget they have a brain?'

A laugh escaped her at that. 'You tell me. You're a man, aren't you?'

'How do you pull the wool over their eyes? Can't they see what you are?'

Laura shook her head. 'Apparently only you have twenty-twenty vision,' she drawled mockingly. 'Of course, it might just be you're the one who's wrong,' she added tauntingly.

He laughed. 'You wish.'

Oh, well, she hadn't really expected him to accept that. Quinn Mannion was a man of strong opinions. It would take dynamite to change his mind about her.

'Why weren't you at the funeral?' he asked her right out of the blue, taking her breath away.

'Excuse me?'

Quinn straightened up, raking a hand through his hair. 'If you were so fond of Alex, why weren't you at his funeral?' he repeated obligingly.

'I was there,' she returned evenly.

His eyes narrowed. 'Nobody saw you,' he countered, clearly thinking she was making it up.

'I'm not devoid of feeling, you know. I knew my presence would be unwelcome, so I didn't go to the graveside.' She had sheltered under a tree some way away, waiting for the family to leave, then she had said her farewells to her father alone. From her vantage point, she now knew there had been one notable absence. 'You weren't there, though.'

Quinn half turned away from her. 'No, I wasn't there,' he confirmed, the tension in his shoulders telling her how much he regretted it.

'Why not?' she asked carefully, doubting he would answer her, but he did.

'I wasn't there because I had no idea Alex was dead,' he admitted tersely, the words emerging hard and scratchy. 'When I'm working, I prefer to be incommunicado. I turn off the phones and the fax, and don't answer the door. My mail can lie unanswered for weeks.' Hands on hips, he stared out over the frozen landscape. 'By the time I eventually found out, the funeral was long over.'

Laura caught her breath. She felt the pain behind the confession, and knew that he would never forgive himself for not knowing. She reacted instinctively, standing and reaching out to place a comforting hand on his arm. 'I'm sorry,' she commiserated gently, and felt him tense.

The next instant he had turned and was staring down at her serious expression with a harsh glitter in his eye, and shrugged. 'The last person I want or need sympathy from is you. Or do you seriously think that this little sideshow will get you what you want from me?'

Laura released him as if she had been stung, the colour draining from her cheeks. 'That was uncalled for,' she said in a choked voice and, much to her surprise, Quinn dragged a hand through his hair and let out a breath.

'You're right, it was uncalled for. I apologise.'

'Accepted,' she responded stiffly, glancing away from him. She didn't know why—when she knew what he thought of her—his accusation should have hurt so much, but it had all the same.

Along the shore she saw Tom gesticulating in their direction and then the way they had been going.

'Uh-oh. I think this could be my fault,' Quinn confessed from beside her, and she found herself glancing his way. 'I told Tom about some arrowheads I found here when I was a boy,' he enlarged as Jonathan shepherded the two disgruntled children back to them.

'I don't believe it. Quinn Mannion confessing to a fault!' she scoffed.

'Tell him, Uncle Quinn,' Tom urged the second they were in hearing distance. 'Tell him about the arrowheads.' He jerked his finger at the man who had become an instant enemy for spoiling his fun.

'Yes, tell him, Uncle Quinn,' Laura taunted sardonically, and Quinn sent her a quelling look.

'It's true,' he told Jonathan wryly.

'Told you!' Tom grumbled.

'That may be so,' Jonathan countered, 'but he didn't tell you to go and look for another one on your own, did he?'

Tom scuffed his booted foot against the rocky shore. 'Gee, we weren't going far!'

Quinn hunkered down in front of his nephew. 'It's not the distance, Tom. Anything could have happened to you, and Jonathan would never forgive himself if you got hurt when he was looking after you. Understand?'

'I guess so,' Tom said in a small voice. 'I'm sorry, Uncle Jonathan.'

'That's OK, Tom,' Jonathan accepted, ruffling the boy's hair.

'Aren't we going to look for treasure?' Ellie asked, her face starting to break up in disappointment, and Laura reached out to touch her cheek.

'Of course you are, sweetie. Uncle Quinn is going to take you,' she declared, and both children perked up immediately, looking expectantly at their uncle.

'We'll all go,' Quinn decided. 'Laura was just saying

how much she enjoyed digging for gold,' he added with a sidelong look her way.

'Gold!' Tom yelped, and Laura glared at his uncle.

'Ignore him, Tom. It's just your uncle's idea of a joke. Come on, Uncle Quinn, show us the way,' she urged mockingly.

With a look that promised retribution at some later date, Quinn led the way along the shoreline for a couple of hundred yards, then headed down a clearly marked track into the trees. A short while later he stopped in a small clearing and declared this was the place. Jonathan found sticks for the children and set them to scraping away in a likely spot. Quinn handed a much larger stick to Laura.

'You too.'

She took it gingerly. 'What am I looking for, precisely?'

He grinned, rocking back on his heels. 'Anything which looks vaguely arrow-shaped.'

'Very helpful,' she drawled wryly, overcome by the first natural smile she had seen from him all afternoon. It had quite taken her breath away. 'Are there really any arrowheads here?' she asked doubtfully.

'I haven't the faintest idea,' he admitted unrepentantly. 'But the kids will enjoy grubbing around just the same.'

'And where do you suggest I look?'

'Anywhere you want; just look out for bears.'

Shock swept through her. 'Bears? Are you telling me you get bears here?' she asked in alarm and he laughed, a full throaty sound which she felt all the way to her toes.

'Don't worry, you're too skinny to make a decent

meal!' he told her, turning away, and she glared at his back, realising he had taken her for a ride.

Though she didn't expect to find anything, she shrugged and gave it her best shot. She brushed fallen leaves aside and scraped away at any loose soil, and found several interesting stones but no arrowheads. So centred was she on her own search, it came as a shock to look up some time later and discover she was alone. Her heart fluttered as she wondered how far she had wandered. Yet she was sure she was still in sight of the clearing, only nobody else appeared to be about.

'Hey?' she called out squeakily, and hastily cleared her throat before trying again. 'Anyone there?' The possibility of being lost made her heart quail.

To her relief a voice answered. Right then it didn't matter that it belonged to Quinn.

'Over here,' he called out, and she hurried towards the sound of his voice. Or where she thought it was.

'Where are you?' she queried, unable to see a soul.

'Down here,' his disembodied voice told her, and she rounded a holly bush and found herself looking down into a deep ditch. Quinn stood at the bottom, looking up at her. 'What's up?'

Feeling silly now that she realised she wasn't lost, she shrugged. 'Er…nothing. Where are the others?'

He nodded to his left. 'The ground slopes away over the other side, too. They're probably in the ditch over there. Listen.'

From a distance she could hear the sound of children's laughter, and the deeper sound of Jonathan talking. If anything, it made her feel even more foolish.

'Did you think we'd all gone and left you?' he asked next, much to her consternation.

'No,' she denied instantly, and he grinned.

'Liar!' he taunted, and she was tempted to throw her stick at him. 'Why don't you come down and join me? I promise not to lose you.'

It was an offer she would have given her eye teeth to refuse but, having already had one scare, she wasn't inclined to put herself in line for another. The slope was slippery with dead leaves, but she did all right until almost at the bottom. Then her foot slipped on a hidden rock and she pitched forward with a cry of alarm. Quinn caught her with ease, sweeping her up close against his firm body, holding her breathtakingly tight.

Laura found her face pressed into the curve of his neck and, as she breathed in, the scent of him bombarded her senses. It was a heady mixture which tantalised her. Her knees turned to water and the world faded away, so that all she could hear was the ragged sound of their mingled breathing and the rapid beat of her heart. Her body stirred, her breasts aching as they surged towards him. Pressed so close together as they were, it was impossible to ignore the stirring of Quinn's body, too.

Her stomach clenched on a wave of desire, and she couldn't stop herself moving against him. He groaned, the sound sending a rush of excitement through her. Her head fell back until she was looking up into heated blue eyes, and saw there the same craving she felt. The need to know the feel of his mouth on hers.

'To hell with it!' he growled, and his head slowly began to lower.

Her eyes flickered to his lips and she experienced a dizzying anticipation. His mouth found hers, and at the first brush of his lips she was plunged headlong into a whirlpool of sensation. White heat arced between them, taking her breath away, and it was with a moan of pleasure that she felt his hand slide into her hair, angling her head the better to plunder her mouth.

Laura felt incandescent with longing. His kiss was everything she had ever expected, and more. The touch of his mouth was electric, every brush of his lips like being licked by flame. Her blood sang in her ears and her senses went into overload. Her breath caught on a gasp of delight as Quinn's tongue traced the fullness of her bottom lip, then took advantage of the way her lips parted to thrust its way inside. She went up in flames but didn't care. All she could think of was kissing him back.

She felt Quinn shudder as she responded to the heady pleasure he evoked. Then her tongue found his, and the sensual duel drove them on. She struggled to get her arms free and then flung them around his neck, holding onto the only stable entity in her universe. She felt his body surge against her as his arms tightened convulsively, and whimpered as her own body began to throb with need. Then his thigh insinuated itself between hers, and the pleasure was so great she had to tear her mouth away from his and gasp in air.

The small respite brought with it the cold air of sanity. Laura was amazed at how quickly she had been swept away. The result had been devastating. She was shaking so badly from reaction that she wasn't at all sure she could stand up unaided. Yet she knew it would be a serious mistake to let Quinn know she had been less than in full control.

Flushed and panting, she smiled up at him. 'Well, now. That was interesting,' she murmured huskily. 'Do you want to try having nothing to do with me again?'

The look he shot her as he stepped away was cold enough to freeze ice. 'You want to watch that smart tongue of yours, or I'll put you over my knee and spank you!' Quinn advised in a gravelly voice.

'Ooh, sounds a little kinky, but I'm game if you are!' she snapped right back, and his eyes narrowed dangerously.

'Keep it up, sweetheart, and you'll be laughing on the other side of your face,' he warned, and Laura knew when it was wise to be cautious. However, she wasn't about to let it all go by unremarked.

'Why are you angry with me? I didn't force you to kiss me, Quinn. That was your decision.' And what a devastating decision it had been!

Hands on hips, he stared at her, unable to deny it. 'Yeah, one of my worst,' he agreed disgustedly. 'But it isn't going to happen again.'

'Famous last words. We'll have to wait and see, won't we?' she taunted softly.

Quinn combed his fingers through his hair. 'You'll be waiting till hell freezes over,' he declared, but she merely smiled, knowing it would really annoy him.

'Uncle Qui-in!' Tom's voice floated to them from a distance.

'Over here, Tom,' Quinn called out, then gave her one final word of warning. 'Stay away from me, Laura.'

Her eyebrows arched. 'Scared you'll succumb?' she goaded, and his eyes positively gleamed with anger.

'Don't say another word, or so help me...' He left the threat hanging in the air between them.

Footsteps sounded, and Laura waved as Tom appeared at the top of the slope. The others were close behind him, and there was no time after that for her to analyse all that had happened. Only when they were heading home again, Quinn in the lead giving Tom a piggyback, was she able to mull over the incredible moment.

Her smile grew cat-like with satisfaction. She had him. For all his dislike of her, he had been unable to ignore the need to kiss her. Of course, it hadn't been her intention to get caught up in the process, too. Not that she could help it. The attraction was incredibly powerful. Almost overwhelming. For a while there, she had lost all sense of self. Hell's bells! Nothing like that had ever happened to her before. She was still trembling from the power of it even now. It was the most incredible thing.

She glanced his way, and felt her stomach tighten in instantaneous reaction. Lord, but he was the most exciting man she had ever met. He was also her most dangerous adversary. She would have to be very careful if she intended carrying on with her plan. And she did intend to carry on. This was only the beginning.

Yes, in future she would have to be very, very careful. She had got away with it today, but she could not trust to luck. He had been too angry with himself to take in the fact that she had not been pretending to respond but had, in fact, been as caught up as he had been. Next time—and there would be a next time—she would have to remain cool-headed and fully in control.

She ignored the tiny warning voice which tried to tell her she was biting off more than she could chew. That Quinn Mannion was not the man to take this lying down. She could smell victory, and she was going for it.

CHAPTER FIVE

THE reason for Quinn's absence from lunch was explained soon after they returned to the house. He disappeared almost immediately, only to return with a large Christmas tree which he set in the bay window. Of course, everyone had to help trim it. Even Caroline, who was feeling much better after her quiet afternoon. Laura was pleased to see that both Stella and Philip joined in the fun, their cares for the moment held at bay. Ellie was held up so that she could put the angel on the top, and Tom had the privilege of switching on the lights.

Laura looked on, heart contracting with envy. Whilst it was good to see the family come together, it only served to remind her that she was on the outside. She didn't know how to change that. A week ago she had been certain she knew the way, but now she wasn't so sure. Stella and Philip were so hostile. Naively, she knew she hadn't been expecting that.

She wasn't aware that Maxine had come to join her until she spoke.

'Is anything wrong?' the older woman asked and, when Laura shot her a startled look, smiled faintly. 'Your thoughts seemed far from pleasant.'

Laura laughed uncomfortably. 'I was just thinking how much I would like to belong to a family like yours,' she admitted truthfully.

'You don't have a family?' Maxine enquired with polite interest, watching the antics of the children in amusement.

All of a sudden there appeared an unexpected opening for her to reveal the truth, and Laura's heart did a somersault as she tried to decide whether to take it or not. To tell or not to tell. She hesitated. Now that the moment was there, she had doubts. Which was ridiculous. She was here for this very purpose. She would be a fool to waste the opportunity.

'Actually,' she began, but then made the mistake of looking into the other woman's shadowed eyes. The instant she did that, her nerve failed her. She couldn't do it. Not right now. This woman was not in good health. What if what she had to say caused Maxine to be ill? Laura would never forgive herself if that happened. She wanted to be liked and accepted, not rejected.

'Yes?' Maxine prompted innocently, and Laura licked her lips.

Sighing, she let the moment pass. 'My mother died about a year ago now, and my father...' Her throat closed over. As always when she thought of him, she felt a welling of emotion, and her eyes took on the glitter of suppressed tears. 'He died just recently,' she finally managed to say in a constricted voice.

'I'm so sorry to hear that,' Maxine responded, her compassion instinctive and honest. 'You must miss them both terribly.'

Laura was almost undone by her kindness. A lump rose in her throat, and she had to frown heavily to keep her emotions in check. Yet she felt compelled to say something reassuring to this woman who had offered her understanding, when it must have been the last thing she wanted to do.

'Mrs Harrington,' she said hastily, before she could think better of it. 'I just want you to know that your husband and I never... That is to say, Alexander wasn't...' Realising she was doing a bad job of it, Laura took a deep breath and plunged in. 'We were not lovers, Mrs Harrington, no matter what the press hinted. I just want you to know that,' she finished, looking the other woman squarely in the eye.

Maxine Harrington had gone pale, her eyes searching Laura's to check if she was telling the truth. Apparently whatever she saw there convinced her, for she nodded slowly. 'Thank you for telling me that, Laura. I never doubted my husband, but I have to say it is a great deal off my mind to hear you say it,' she said, then, much to Laura's horror, clutched her hand to her chest and swayed alarmingly.

'Mrs Harrington?' she cried sharply, her words carrying across the room, making the others look round quickly.

'I just feel a little dizzy,' Maxine declared faintly, collapsing into the nearest chair.

They were surrounded in seconds.

'Mother?' Stella said anxiously, as Laura felt hard fingers close on her arm, drawing her away. She found herself looking up into Quinn's inimitable face.

'What did you say to her?' he demanded in a furious undertone, and Laura swiftly shook her head.

'Nothing,' she insisted, feeling quite sick with dread that she might be responsible for heaven knew what.

'It had to be something,' he maintained chillingly, and she bit her lip nervously.

'We were just talking. I swear I never said anything to upset her. I wouldn't.'

Glacial blue eyes never gave an inch. 'How the hell are we supposed to know what you would or wouldn't do?'

'Because if Laura said it was so, then it was,' Jonathan

declared hardily, materialising at her side and slipping an arm around her shoulders. Quinn eyed the gesture narrowly.

'Easy for you to say, Jon, but why should I trust her?' he growled out, and his friend sent him a level look.

'That's something only you can decide,' Jonathan returned smoothly, 'but I've always found that in order to trust you have to be willing to do so. It's an act of faith.'

Quinn took a deep breath, his eyes scanning Laura's pale face. 'You're asking a lot,' he muttered, and Jonathan smiled faintly.

'Nobody said it was easy.'

Into the small silence which fell, Maxine's exasperated voice was clearly audible.

'I'll be perfectly fine if you all stop fussing. All I need is a rest.'

Laura turned to the other woman as she stood up, and Maxine, though still pale, looked wryly amused. However, seeing Laura's concern, she reached out and touched her hand. 'Thank you. I appreciate your kindness,' she said again. Then Stella was by her side, cutting off any reply Laura might have wanted to make.

'I'll help you to your room, Mother.'

Swallowing, Laura folded her arms and bit down hard on her lip to stop it trembling. At least she had done something right. Maxine would never have asked. She still had not sought more clarification. Perhaps, given time, she might be ready to hear the whole truth. Laura certainly hoped so. After Maxine's reaction to something quite small, she would have to be ultra-careful about dropping her bombshell.

Quinn frowned after his godmother, then looked sharply at Laura. 'What was that all about?'

Laura rubbed wearily at her forehead. She had had all

she could take of Quinn Mannion for now. 'If you really want to know, ask Mrs Harrington. I'm sure you'll take her word more readily than mine,' she said tiredly. 'Now, if you'll both excuse me, I'm going to go up to my room and take a long, relaxing bath.'

As it turned out, the bath was certainly long, but far from relaxing, because her mind had a tendency to keep drifting over those heady moments in the wood. Reliving them, she discovered, was almost as exciting as the original encounter. Consequently, when she did climb out of the scented water, she was feeling extremely restless.

It was a sensation which stayed with her until she went down to dinner, and then it magically vanished when she took her seat beside Quinn at the table. It took her to dessert to realise what had happened and make the connection. She always felt more alive when she was around him. He stimulated her mind, and she had to think fast on her feet to keep ahead of him. She was actually looking forward to crossing swords with him again, which was strange, considering she disliked him so much. But then, she didn't have to like him to fight him.

After dinner, as it was Christmas Eve, the children were allowed to stay up and open just one present from the pile which had magically appeared under the tree. Then Ellie disappeared, returning a few minutes later with a large picture book. She climbed up onto Quinn's lap, made herself comfortable, and presented the book for him to read.

Sitting on a couch with Caroline and Jonathan, Laura looked on with the strangest sensation in her chest as he read to the little girl. It was almost as if it were being squeezed by invisible fingers. She found herself holding her breath.

'Twas the night before Christmas, when all through the house, not a creature was stirring, not even a mouse.'

'Quinn would make a good father,' Caroline said wistfully. 'He always has time for these two when he visits. He ought to have a family of his own.'

Laura had been thinking exactly the same thing. 'For that he would have to have a wife,' she pointed out, and Caroline grimaced.

'It's not as if he doesn't have the chance. Lord knows, he goes out with enough women!'

'Perhaps that's it. He's spoilt for choice,' she joked, though it gave her the oddest feeling to think of Quinn married.

Caroline sighed. 'It's not that. He doesn't trust women. Not many people know that he was engaged once, years ago. Tonia was a bitch; she took him for a ride. She didn't love him, just his money. When Quinn found out she was seeing other men... Well, he was so angry it scared me. I thought he was going to kill her. He changed overnight. He went from being this warm, caring man to a cynical, distrustful stranger. Oh, not with us, his family, but with women. Though I hate to say it, he uses them. Not in an unkind way. He's very generous with gifts and things which cost money, but he never gives his heart. It's as if he's walled it up somewhere. Sometimes I think he needs to be shaken up a bit. It would do him good to want a woman who doesn't want him. Not that I want to see him hurt,' she put in quickly, 'but...I despair for him sometimes, I really do.'

Laura frowned, allowing her gaze to linger on Quinn. What Caroline said explained a lot. It didn't excuse all his behaviour, but it did show her why he was so ready to believe the worst. Experience had predisposed him to do so. She could see the man he had used to be as he was holding Ellie. He had all the gentleness of a strong man. It was a shame he had chosen to lock his heart away because of one evil woman.

She shifted uncomfortably. Not that she was interested in his heart. She hated waste in all its forms. Even when it came in the shape of a man like Quinn.

When Quinn finished reading. Caroline stood up. 'OK, you two, time for bed,' she declared in a no-nonsense voice.

'Aw, Mom!' Tom complained noisily. 'It's too early.'

Quinn rose with Ellie in his arms. 'The sooner you get to sleep, the sooner Santa Claus will come,' he said, by way of inducement. 'Come on, I'll come up with you.'

Not long after he had disappeared with Caroline and the children, Laura excused herself too. She wasn't tired, but she did have a lot to think about. However, as she reached the bottom of the stairs, her eyes caught the soft glow of light coming from the door opposite. Jonathan had told her that the room had been Alexander's study, and all at once Laura had the urge to see it. To explore the room in which her father had spent so much of his time.

Feeling like a thief, she glanced behind her, but no-body was watching. In the space of a heartbeat she was across the floor and through the door. The light came from a lamp set on the desk which graced one end of the book-lined room. A comfortable reading chair sat by the empty grate and Laura crossed to it, running her hands gently over the soft leather surface. She could imagine her father sitting here, reading a much thumbed book whilst sipping at some of his favourite Napoleon brandy.

She sighed heavily, wishing for things which just could not be, and crossed to the desk. It lay as it had done since Alexander had last used it. A moment trapped in time. A framed photograph sat at one corner and she picked it up, studying it wistfully. It was of the family, all laughing into the camera. She set it back down again carefully and wandered over to the nearest bookcase, picking out a volume at random and flicking through the pages.

Suddenly the hairs on the back of her neck stood up, but before she even had time to tense a voice spoke from right behind her.

'Snooping?'

Laura spun round, dropping the book onto the carpet as she stared up into Quinn's brooding face.

'I thought you were upstairs,' she gasped, then wished she had kept quiet for the words made her sound guilty as hell. Which, of course, she was. She knew as well as he did that she shouldn't be in here without permission.

'You thought wrong,' he countered, bending to retrieve the book and slot it back in place. The action brought him heart-stoppingly close to her, and Laura drew in a ragged breath. 'What were you hoping to find in here?' he asked softly, staring down into her startled eyes.

Her senses were still heightened from that afternoon and his nearness, with the memory so clear in her mind, was sending her breathing haywire. 'Nothing,' she said, trying to sound unconcerned.

Those amazingly blue eyes quartered her face, tracing her features like a caress. They stopped at her mouth, and her lips parted on a swift intake of breath. She wished he would either step back or step closer. He was tantalisingly poised in between, and it set her nerves jangling like crazy.

'Nothing?' he charged sceptically, raising his eyes to hers again.

There was something at the back of those eyes which gave her pause, then she realised what it was. Interest. Though he was trying to hide it, it was there. Just like her, he was remembering that passionate kiss they had shared. His mind might not want to know her, but his body had other ideas. Inside, he was fighting a battle with himself, but he was a strong-willed man and was bound to win, unless she brought up reinforcements against him. Her pulse skittered at the very idea, but something stronger urged her on.

'I haven't taken anything, but you don't have to take my word for it. You can always search me,' she suggested provocatively, raising her arms away from her body, whilst her heart lurched at her daring. It was a bluff. She didn't want him to touch her, because she knew the power he had over her senses would tip the balance back in his favour. No, she just wanted to taunt him.

His eyes skipped over the way her calf-length black dress hugged her figure, setting her body tingling. She saw his jaw flex, and told herself he wouldn't call her bluff.

'You love to live dangerously, don't you?' he murmured, and shocked her to the core by reaching out and placing a hand on either side of her midriff, within a hair's breadth of her breasts. The heat of his touch was like being licked by flame and her breasts surged against the restriction of her clothes, her nipples hardening into tight points which pressed against the soft fabric.

Now his eyes locked on hers, and suddenly there didn't seem to be nearly enough air in the room.

One eyebrow quirked. 'Ready?' he asked with husky softness, and her body tightened on a pulse of desire.

She knew she ought to back off, but couldn't. Her mouth had gone so dry, it was hard to get words out. 'Go ahead,' she said tautly, bracing herself for what she knew would be a supreme form of torture: the slow glide of his hands over her.

Quinn's fingers flexed, but remained still. 'You'd let me do it, too, wouldn't you?'

'I'm always open to new experiences. I've never been searched before. I'm sure I'll enjoy it,' she managed to respond audaciously, knowing she would have nobody to blame but herself if he took her up on it.

'I'm sure you would,' he agreed dulcetly, and her eyes were drawn to his mouth which hovered so tantalisingly close to her own.

Suddenly she wanted quite desperately to feel the touch of his lips on hers. She knew it would be another stunning experience. The sense of expectancy was electrifying and she moistened her lips with the tip of her tongue. Hearing a muffled groan, she glanced up. Quinn was staring at her mouth with such hunger in his gaze, her whole body clenched with an answering desire.

'You have a mouth which just begs to be kissed,' Quinn remarked thickly, and she couldn't have moved away right then if she had wanted to. She forgot that it was not for real. All she knew was that she would die if he didn't kiss her.

'Kiss me, then,' she sighed, her hands coming to rest on his chest, feeling the heat of his body and the loud thud of his heart. Quinn's fingers tightened, drawing her inexorably closer as his head started to lower. A soft groan got trapped in her throat. Her heart stopped beating.

She was totally unprepared for him to let her go and step away from her.

'Inviting as the offer is, I'll pass this time,' he said, eyes glinting sardonically down at her, and her heart kicked as she realised he hadn't been as caught up as she had believed. He had lured her in and sprung his own trap.

Desperately needing to hide her crushing sense of disappointment, Laura leant back against the bookcase with every appearance of calm, when in truth her legs were trembling and she needed the support. 'Spoilsport,' she charged mockingly.

His lips curled. 'Nice try.'

She shrugged. 'I'm glad you liked it.'

A husky laugh escaped him. 'Oh, you're nothing if not entertaining.'

She cocked her head to one side, and smiled alluringly. 'Admit it. You were tempted.'

Quinn shook his head wryly. 'Go to bed, Laura.'

Pushing herself upright, she was glad to feel her legs support her. 'Oh, well, you can't win them all,' she sighed, heading for the door without a backward glance.

Safely in her room, Laura let out a frustrated groan. Damn, but he was as slippery as a fish. Just when she'd thought she had him, he had turned the tables, and she had come close to showing him she was far from being in control herself. Not that she imagined he would do anything with the knowledge, but knowing he knew would be humiliating. She had been very fortunate tonight.

She showered and got ready for bed, but sleep seemed to be beyond her. A dull throb behind her eyes warned her of an impending headache, so she took two pain-killers, then curled up against the pillows in her silk pyjamas. It had been quite a visit so far. The last thing she had expected when she'd come here was to find herself lusting after Quinn Mannion.

Her mind was filled with images of him, both angry and aroused. Every time they touched she was caught up in a whirlwind of sensations, and the effect was getting stronger. She ought to be alarmed, but she wasn't. Uppermost was a kind of reckless excitement. She couldn't help wondering what it would be like to be made love to by Quinn.

Of course, it would never happen. The man had the worst possible opinion of her. Never mind that she had actively encouraged that opinion; he had made his mind up before he met her. Had the situation been different, she might have enjoyed discovering the possibilities but, whilst Quinn thought of her the way he did, it was out of the question.

She mulled on that and many other things over the next few hours whilst she waited for sleep to claim her. Eventually, at close to two in the morning, she sighed and accepted defeat. At least the pills she had taken for her headache had worked. But elusive sleep was still a million miles away. She finally decided that a milky drink might help. At least it wouldn't hurt, and it would give her something to do instead of lying in bed awake.

Climbing from the bed, she slipped her feet into slippers and padded out of the room. She didn't bother with a robe, for the house was warm and she didn't expect to run into anybody at this hour. Except, perhaps, Santa Claus, and she didn't expect he would say anything about how she was dressed.

Downstairs she made her way to the breakfast room

which would give her access to the kitchen. Opening the kitchen door, she stepped inside and searched for the light switch. Flicking it on, it gave her a terrible shock to discover she was not alone. Sitting at the table, squinting against the sudden glare of light, was Quinn. Laura nearly screamed and her hand did rise to her throat, only to stop there when she recognised him.

'What were you doing sitting in the dark?' she yelped, alarm only slowly slipping away, but its passing didn't slow down the rapid beat of her heart. She was very much aware of her state of *déshabillé*, and felt alarmingly unprotected and at a distinct disadvantage.

'Not sleeping, and the kitchen seemed as good a place as any to do it in!' he informed her dryly, and she stared at him, finally seeing him properly.

There was a lot to see, for Quinn was dressed in jeans—and nothing else. Everything above his waist was bare, like his feet. Oh, Lord! Her mouth went dry at the sight of the tanned expanse of his torso. She was right. There wasn't an ounce of spare flesh on him. The breadth of his shoulders invited touch, and her fingertips tingled with a sudden and insistent need to do so. His dark hair was a mess, as if he had tossed and turned for ages before coming down here.

Deep inside her a throbbing started up, and she felt the slow pulse of her blood as it heated in her veins. Suddenly the room was too small, too hot and Quinn far too close.

'Couldn't you have put something more on?' she complained huskily, and could have bitten her tongue out as she realised just how revealing the question was.

'This is more than I was wearing before I came down here,' he pointed out in some amusement as his eyes travelled over the fetching look of her in her silky pyjamas, which were just a little too long in the arm and leg and made her look both vulnerable and heart-stoppingly sensual at the same time. 'Very nice. Very sexy,' he complimented softly. 'If you wore those pyjamas for my benefit, they did the trick. You have my undivided attention.'

Laura's thoughts had been centred on the erotic vision of an unabashedly naked Quinn in his bed, but they were drawn back by that comment. She didn't particularly want his undivided attention right now; she was far too aware of him as it was. It was one thing to play at seduction in daylight and quite another in the dark. She took a steadying breath, knowing that coming down here had been a mistake. One she intended to rectify right away.

'I'd better go,' she said firmly, turning back towards the door.

Quinn rose gracefully to his feet, his hands resting on the low-slung waist of his jeans, which were zipped but not fastened. 'Running away so soon, sweetheart? That doesn't sound like you,' he taunted huskily, and reluctantly she was compelled to turn and face him.

'I never run away from anything or anyone,' she declared, and something alarmingly like satisfaction gleamed in his eyes for a moment, then was gone.

Smiling faintly, Quinn ran a hand over his chest, dragging her gaze helplessly to the magnificent breadth of it. Need was instant. She wanted to touch it, stroke it. Lose herself in the feel of it.

'So, why did you come down here?' he asked, raking a hand through his hair, making her want to do that too. To feel the vibrant tendrils curl about her fingers.

Damn him, he was being deliberately provocative. She knew it as well as she knew her own name. It didn't alter the effect on her, though. Her senses were in such a responsive state, they were positively zinging. She drew in a rather shaky breath, determined to keep her wilful thoughts from straying down dangerous paths.

'I couldn't sleep. I hoped a drink might do the trick,' she explained as coolly as she could.

He laughed softly. 'Drinking won't help. Trust me, I've tried it.'

For the first time she noticed the empty glass on the table.

'Drowning your sorrows?' she couldn't resist goading softly, and he smiled.

'If you want to know the truth, I've been sitting here thinking about you,' he admitted, totally surprising her.

Her eyes widened. 'Me?'

'You. You're giving me quite a headache.'

'Take two aspirin and it will go away,' she suggested flippantly, whilst inside she found it unnerving to think of him thinking of her. She was sure it couldn't be anything good. The day he thought well of her, hell would freeze over.

Quinn rubbed a hand around the back of his neck, easing tensed muscles. 'The headache might go, but you would still be here. I've been trying to decide if the satisfaction of having you would be worth compromising my principles,' he declared shockingly.

Laura blinked, lips parting on a gasp of disbelief. 'What did you say?'

He sent her an old-fashioned look. 'Don't sound so surprised. You knew I wanted you,' he charged sardonically, bringing colour to her cheeks.

Of course she had known. That was what this was all about—making him admit it, by deed as well as word. However, she had not counted on him calmly sitting there deciding whether to have her or not. Of all the nerve!

She folded her arms belligerently. 'Did it ever occur to you that I might not agree to your...having me, as you so quaintly put it?' she asked frostily.

His teeth flashed as he smiled. 'It never crossed my mind,' he drawled, and she gnashed her teeth in impotent fury. Arrogant devil!

'Then you are in for one hell of a shock. The answer is no,' she told him in no uncertain terms. She might want him till her nerves were at fever pitch, but she would never succumb. Never to a man who could think such thoughts.

Quinn abandoned the table and paced towards her, reminding her of a big cat stalking its prey. Her eyes widened. Instinct told her to run, but she wouldn't give him that satisfaction. She knew he was playing games with her for his own amusement, and she refused to let him see he was getting to her.

Coming to a halt scant inches in front of her, he tipped his head to one side. 'No?'

Her chin rose. She refused to be intimidated. 'Absolutely, definitely,' she confirmed, then lost her breath as he braced a hand on the wall at either side of her, blocking her escape. Her heart leapt into her throat.

'Aren't you the least bit curious?' he asked softly, and she swallowed nervously. He was way, way too close, but she couldn't push him away and maintain her credibility. Besides, she had the awful feeling her hands would cling rather than shove.

'Curious about what?' she asked unevenly, so aware of him her nerves screamed at her to close the gap. She had never felt such a sexual pull, one that made it almost painful to remain where she was.

Blue eyes glittered down at her. 'If it would be the same this time,' he told her, and she didn't need him to elaborate. He was talking about that kiss they had shared.

At the mention of it, something wild was released into the room. Something which daylight had kept at bay, but which now roamed untamed in the night-time. The temperature in the room shot off the scale in those few seconds, and Laura found it difficult to breathe. Her heart lurched. The air positively seethed with the power of the elemental attraction which sparked between them.

Of course she wondered, yet she would not admit it to him. She found a flashing smile. 'You know, it never crossed my mind,' she retorted swiftly.

'Liar,' Quinn murmured as he raised a hand and brushed his fingers across her cheek. Instantly all her nerve-endings came alive, and she dragged in air painfully.

'Calling me names won't promote your cause,' she remonstrated, hating the way her voice sounded so husky.

His thumb stroked over her lips. 'What will?' he asked seductively, and she shivered. She would not succumb. She would not!

'You're wasting your time, Quinn,' she declared hardily.

He laughed softly. 'Did you know that even the way you say my name turns me on?' he growled, turning her stomach over.

'Stop playing games,' she ordered as firmly as she could.

'Why? I thought this was your favourite game,' he taunted huskily. 'I thought you wanted me caught up in your trap.'

She was getting quite desperate for him to let her go, and it made her reckless. 'I don't want you at all!' she denied, and he shook his head.

'Now that is a lie I'm just going to have to disprove,' he declared, lowering his head.

Realising her mistake, Laura's hands came up to keep him at bay, but it was no use. Her 'No!' was smothered by the press of his mouth on hers.

It started out as a game; she knew that. He was playing with her and she intended to fight him, but after the first kiss everything changed. It stopped being a game the second their lips touched. Not just for her, but for both of them. She felt his shock as white-hot passion tore through them so swiftly it was dizzying. The last thing she remembered thinking was it *was* the same. Then there was no more time for thought. Within seconds they were deaf to everything but the need they created, and which only they could satisfy. Each scintillating kiss stoked the fire, turning it into a conflagration. She couldn't get close enough, and neither, apparently, could Quinn.

With a groan Quinn's arms went round her, pulling her close to the solid strength of his body. Laura sighed as his hands glided down her back, closing on her hips and lifting her until she felt the swell of his arousal. She moved against him instinctively, and trembled when his hand found the hem of her pyjama jacket and slipped beneath it. His hands were hot on the tender skin of her back, gliding upwards then round until his thumbs caressed the underside of her breasts.

Her head fell back as Quinn completed his devastation by capturing her breast. Laura felt herself swell into his hand, the engorged nub pressing into his palm. His thumb stroked her mercilessly, teasing her until she groaned, then his head lowered and his mouth claimed her through the silk of her jacket. She cried out then, her fingers curling into the flesh of his shoulder as he suckled her. Sensation after sensation tore through her, tossing her pellmell into that stormy sea of passion.

She clung on, her own hands moving restlessly over the bronzed skin of his shoulders. But she needed more than just to take; she wanted to give. Her fingers curled into his hair, tugging his head up until she was able to press her mouth to the hollow of his throat. She licked him, and it was Quinn's turn to groan as she slipped her arms around him and ran her nails down his back. She felt the denim of his jeans block her path, but she didn't allow it to deter her. Her hands slipped beneath it, her fingers tightening on his firm buttocks.

There seemed to be only one possible outcome. Such a powerful need had to be satisfied. Neither was thinking of consequences as Quinn urged her towards the table. They staggered into it, and unknown to either of them the empty glass fell over and rolled towards the edge. It was the sound of breaking glass as it hit the floor which brought her back to reality.

'Forget about it,' Quinn muttered hoarsely, burying his face in her neck and trailing kisses down to where her pulse beat rapidly.

Laura wanted to ignore it, but she couldn't. The spell had been broken. Realisation of what she had been about to do was like plunging into cold water. Was she insane? However much she wanted this man, he despised her. How could she have forgotten that to the point of almost allowing him to make love to her?

'Stop!' she gasped out, pushing at his shoulders, but he ignored her. 'Damn it, Quinn, I said stop!' she cried louder, and he swore, going quite still. Seconds later he pushed her to arm's length and stared at her, frowning, breathing heavily.

'What are you, some kind of witch? What spell have you put on me that I can't keep my hands off you?' he asked angrily, sending a jolt clean through her at the unexpected admission.

It cut through the sense of self-disgust she had been feeling at her inability to resist him. He had given her an opening to salve her pride, and she didn't waste a second using it to her advantage. She had to hide the fact that she had been as swept away as he had been, and at the same time she had to make sure he would keep her at arm's length in future. Those heated moments in his arms had proved to her she could not trust herself anywhere near him.

Though it took some nerve, she reached out and traced a finger through the fine dark hair on his chest. 'I'm just a woman. A woman you want. The question is, how much do you want me? I think this would be a good time to talk terms, don't you?' she asked silkily, willing her heart to cease its crazy racing.

His eyes fastened on hers, anger dying, to be replaced by an almost unnatural calm. He released her with exaggerated care, stepping back so that her hand fell away. 'Terms?'

The relief at his letting her go was enormous. So far so good. Now, if she could just tweak a nerve or two… 'Uh-huh. You didn't expect to get something for nothing, did you?' she asked in amusement. 'That kiss was just something on account. If you want more of the same, you're going to have to offer me something in return. Let's call it a quid pro quo,' she told him with a cool smile, and waited, scarcely breathing, for his response. He ought to be furious.

Quinn was so still, he could have put a statue to shame. 'Let me get this right. You expect me to pay for the privilege of having you?' he asked with deceptive softness.

A shiver chased its way down her spine. His calmness was unnerving. By rights he should be spitting nails. Why wasn't he? 'Surely you didn't expect anything else?' she challenged with a laugh.

Quinn crossed his arms, regarding her with narrowed eyes. 'I could have had you for nothing just then,' he declared bluntly, making her nerves jolt at the unnecessary reminder. That wasn't quite what she had wanted him to say.

'I think not,' she denied, unable to do anything else.

'I think yes. I know when a woman is aroused. You were out of control, sweetheart. If that glass hadn't fallen, we would still be making love right there on the kitchen table,' Quinn replied, setting her heart thumping anxiously.

Laura knew she couldn't deny it. She would only make herself ridiculous. It was a case of shame the devil. She forced herself to meet his eyes. 'You're a good lover, Quinn, and I admit to being a little caught up. A mistake on my part. I won't be making it again.'

Something fierce flashed in his eyes. 'You went up like dry tinder. What makes you think you would respond any differently next time?'

Damn. This wasn't going quite the way she had intended. He was supposed to be put off, not challenged. She would have to try harder. 'Because you won't get to sample the goods unless you pay for them first!' she retorted brazenly, certain that would do the trick. 'And, whilst we're on the subject, I don't come cheap,' she added for good measure.

A slow smile, which was not quite pleasant, crossed his lips. 'I take it the terms are non-negotiable?' Quinn drawled, and she shivered again.

'I never negotiate,' she confirmed, staring him out.

'Neither do I,' he countered smoothly, and Laura decided this was definitely the moment when a wise general made a tactical retreat.

She called upon all the sang-froid at her disposal and made her way to the door. Opening it, she glanced at him over her shoulder. 'I'll leave you to think it over. Goodnight, Quinn, darling. Sleep well,' she cooed and, stepping outside, shut the door firmly.

With the solid piece of wood between them, she was tempted to sag against it, but there was always the chance that Quinn would follow her. If he found her there in a state of near collapse he would soon guess something wasn't on the level. So, on legs which threatened to give way at every step, she retraced the route to her room. Only there did she collapse onto the edge of the bed and close her eyes.

Dear God, that had been close! She had escaped by the skin of her teeth. She hadn't been in control of the situation from the moment she'd stepped into the kitchen and found Quinn there. Events had controlled her. When the wisest course had been to leave, she had stayed. Compounding the error by almost allowing him to make love to her.

But she had recovered her position. At least...she hoped she had. His response had been...odd. She hadn't expected him to take her demands as a challenge. A frisson of alarm shimmered over her skin. She admitted to being concerned, but what could he really do? He certainly wouldn't pay, and she doubted he would even want to touch her again.

Which was just as well, considering. Her ability to resist him ranked on a par with the seasonal rainfall in the desert: almost zero. The best way to keep her head was to keep her distance. Hopefully, her ultimatum had solved that problem.

She groaned, flinging herself back onto the dishevelled bed. Lord, but the man was pure temptation. She had to be crazy to want him so much, when she knew what he thought of her. Yet there was no denying it. Every time he touched her, she was in danger of forgetting everything but the way he could make her feel. And that, under the circumstances, was downright dangerous.

CHAPTER SIX

IT HAD snowed overnight. Somewhere between the time she returned to her room and morning, the world had turned white and silent. From her vantage point by the window, Laura stared out at the snowy scene with less than her customary pleasure. She was tense, and she knew why. Quinn. Her first look at his face ought to tell her of her success or failure, but she hadn't seen him yet this morning. He had already breakfasted by the time she came down.

Behind her the family was gathered to open their presents. Despite Alexander's absence, or maybe because of it, everyone was in a determinedly festive mood. They were grouped around Maxine like soldiers guarding the colours. There was no place for her in their midst. She hadn't expected there to be, but it was a painful reminder of how alone she was. And how very much she wanted to belong.

She could hear the children's excited exclamations as each parcel was unwrapped, and smiled at their unbridled exuberance. How simple everything was when you were young. As a child she had always enjoyed this part of the day, still did, though now she preferred giving presents rather than just receiving them. She had already given Jonathan the engraved pen she had bought him. He had given her a recipe book. It had been out of print for many years, and it warmed her to think of the trouble he must have gone to to find it for her, knowing her love for cooking.

Sighing, she opened the book and flipped through the pages. One particular recipe caught her attention, and the next instant she was engrossed.

'Interesting book?'

Caught up as she was in the intricacies of the dish, Laura hadn't heard Quinn's silent approach. His unexpected question caused her to jump violently, clutching the book to her chest in a purely defensive gesture. Glancing round, she found him standing so close, barely a breath could pass between them.

He was so near, in fact, she could see there was nothing to see. Nothing to tell her the result of their last meeting. All she could say for sure was that his eyes seemed to be an even more piercing shade of blue this morning. They had an immediate effect on her. She felt them swallowing her up whole, and her body suddenly thrummed with such piercingly sensual awareness that an ache started up deep inside her.

'Laura?' Her name was laced with sardonic amusement, and to her consternation she realised she had been caught staring. That wasn't all. She knew he had asked her a question, only she couldn't remember what it was. Faint, betraying colour entered her cheeks as she set about pulling herself together in a hurry.

'I'm sorry. I was miles away. What did you say?' she asked with a tiny shake of her head to get herself thinking straight. Where had her wits gone begging when she needed them most?

Quinn transferred his gaze to the book she still clasped to her bosom. 'I asked if it was an interesting book,' he repeated obligingly reaching out to take it from her. His fingers brushed across her breast in the process, sending her pulse rocketing out of control. She couldn't decide if it had been deliberate or accidental, but it scarcely mattered. The result was the same either way. Her body contracted sharply, the ache expanding.

Apparently oblivious, Quinn was reading the title of the book. His eyebrows rose when he saw what it was. 'Recipes? Don't tell me you can cook!'

She wasn't surprised by his scoffing tone, but she was disturbed as hell by his nearness and by the lack of animosity in his attitude. After last night, she had expected him to keep his distance. This…friendliness was distinctly unsettling.

'I happen to be a very good cook,' she countered calmly, whilst inside she was frantically wishing he would move away because he was setting her nerves jangling. His silent approach had caused her to be neatly trapped between the window and a small table. The only way to get by him was to brush against him and, quite frankly, she didn't want to get that close to him.

'Right. How do you make eggs?' he asked mockingly, and she took the book back, closing it with a snap.

'Personally, I leave that to the chickens,' she drawled with heavy irony, and he laughed, making her sense of unease deepen. This should not be happening. Alarm bells started ringing madly. What was he up to? Clearing her throat, she did her best to seem equally unconcerned. 'Everyone seems to be having fun.'

Quinn glanced round at the laughing group before giving her his full attention once more. 'Feeling left out?'

She was, as it happened, but she knew better than to tell him so. No doubt he would only laugh and tell her it served her right. 'I think everyone would like to be a child again at Christmas.'

'How do you usually spend the holiday? You're hardly the sort of woman a man takes home to his family.'

Ah, now that sounded more like the Quinn she knew. She sent him an old-fashioned look. 'Up until a year ago, I spent it with my mother. We would attend midnight service together. Then on Christmas morning we would go for a long walk whilst dinner was cooking. Afterwards I would nuke some popcorn in the microwave, and we would get through a box of tissues watching *It's A Wonderful Life* on the television. Surprised?'

'Nothing about you surprises me any more,' he replied smoothly. 'It sounds like you'd get along with my mother. She's a sucker for old movies, too,' he added, grinning when she turned a startled gaze on him. 'What's the matter? Didn't you think I had a mother? Did you think I'd sprung to life fully formed?'

'Actually, I was amazed that you would link me with your mother in any way. Did you forget who I was?' she jibed, reminding him that he didn't like her.

'Oh, there's no chance I'd ever forget who you are, sweetheart,' he came back softly, with the cutting edge of a lancet.

It was the first intimation she had of the effect the events of the night had had on him. He sounded coldly furious. It was what she had hoped for, but it made her uneasy all the same. She realised she might just have caught a tiger by the tail.

'You're angry,' she pronounced unnecessarily, and he smiled.

'Oh, I'm nothing so watered down as angry,' he told her conversationally, and goose-flesh danced over her skin. Rather belatedly she realised she had not allowed for the possibility of his seeking some form of retribution.

Before she could formulate a response, however, Maxine spoke.

'Did I hear you mention going to church, Laura? There's a service in town this morning you could attend. I'm sure Quinn will take you if you want to go,' she proposed, much to Laura's surprise and alarm.

The idea was to keep Quinn at a safe distance, not go swanning off into the wilderness with him. Not that she expected he would agree to the proposal. She looked at him, eyebrows raised. 'Oh, I couldn't put him to so much trouble, Mrs Harrington,' she declined, waiting expectantly for him to back her up.

His lips curved faintly. 'It would be no trouble,' he insisted, and Laura blinked at him incredulously.

Her eyes narrowed at the gleam in his. Damn him, he was enjoying her discomfiture. 'I'm sure you must have better things to do,' she urged pointedly, but Quinn slipped his hands into his trouser pockets and eyed her in amusement.

'Not right now.'

'That's settled, then,' Maxine said in satisfaction, but, as she looked at Laura, a frown appeared between her brows. 'I can't understand it. There seems to be something terribly familiar about you, but I know for a fact that we have never met.'

'I said exactly the same thing,' Caroline put in immediately, sending shock waves through Laura. Lord, what if, between them, they made the connection? The very last thing she wanted was for her relationship to Alexander Harrington to come blurting out. It should be done carefully, in private, when she was sure the moment was right. This, she knew, was the wrong time. Needing to divert the two women, she looked to Jonathan for help.

He gave it immediately. 'Laura is a much sought after interior designer, Maxine. No doubt you've seen pictures of her in magazines,' he offered smoothly, and the older woman nodded slowly.

'Yes, that could be it,' she agreed, albeit without total conviction. 'Ah, well, I'm sure it will come to me eventually,' she added with a smile before giving her attention to Ellie who was trying to show her something.

Laura breathed a sigh of relief. She didn't feel any more ready to hear the truth revealed right now than she was sure Maxine was ready to hear it. She silently sent Jonathan her heartfelt thanks for saving her bacon.

'Why don't you want me to take you to church, Laura?' Quinn asked quietly, drawing her attention back to him.

She sent him a sideways look. 'Do you really need to ask? Because I don't trust you,' she told him bluntly. If he was as angry as he'd implied, she would be wise to be cautious.

'In church? Shame on you. What do you possibly think I could do to you there?' he taunted, lips curving into a mocking smile.

Laura eyed him back equally mockingly. 'Just because you're going to church, that doesn't make you a saint!'

He laughed seductively. 'I don't think you'd have any use for a saint, Laura, but I'll tell you what I'll do. I promise not to do anything to alarm you on the way, OK? Does that make you feel safer?'

He was treating her like a five-year-old, and deriving a great deal of amusement in the process. God, he made her want to slap him hard. 'I'll keep you to it,' she agreed, and his amusement deepened. He knew exactly what she had wanted to do and why.

'You do that.'

She looked away from him before she could give in

to temptation. Her eyes fell on the children playing. 'So, tell me, what did Father Christmas bring you, Quinn?' she enquired sardonically.

The change of direction took him by surprise, and Quinn eyed her speculatively. 'I forgot to post my list this year.'

'Poor little boy,' Laura responded sympathetically. 'Didn't you get even one present?'

He shook his head, eyes glittering in a way which set her pulse jumping. 'Not yet, but I expect that to change,' he declared ominously. 'We'd better be going. We don't want to be late.'

Laura reluctantly allowed herself to be steered towards the door. She was more surprised than alarmed when he stopped in the doorway and turned to her.

'There is just one thing,' he murmured, eyes lifting.

Laura followed his gaze, and her stomach fell away. There, tacked just above the doorway, was a bunch of mistletoe. Her eyes widened in sudden comprehension, and shot to Quinn's. The blue orbs sent off glittering sparks as he neatly foiled her attempt to back away.

'No!' she denied, heart fluttering like a trapped butterfly.

'Yes!' he countered, taking her mouth.

She wanted to struggle but, as she raised her hands to fight him off, Tom's excited treble reached her ears.

'Oh, boy! Uncle Quinn's kissing Laura!'

She knew then that everyone in the room had to be watching them, and to engage in an undignified tussle was out of the question. Which had to be what Quinn was counting on. She was compelled to stay still and pray that the kiss would be brief. She should have known better. Quinn had other intentions.

From a distance it probably looked fairly innocuous,

but in reality it was quite the contrary. It was a kiss which took her right back to that knife-edge of excitement. He explored her mouth, using against her the knowledge he had discovered last night. He knew what made her shiver, what made her sigh, and he wanted her to do both. To prove that she had been lying when she'd said she would not be caught again. He wanted to make her eat her words, but she was equally determined to do no such thing.

She refused to give in, though every brush of his lips, every stroke of his tongue drove her crazy. Just when she thought she would have to give in or go mad, he let her go. Breathing hard, she stared up at him defiantly.

Quinn stepped back. 'Merry Christmas, Laura,' he said provocatively, and for the sake of those watching their little tableau she was forced to refrain from boxing his ears.

'Merry Christmas, Quinn,' she responded stonily, and he smiled.

'I'll meet you outside in five minutes,' he advised her, but Laura had had enough.

'I'm not going anywhere with you,' she whispered to him angrily, but, instead of arguing, he turned to the still silent and watchful members of the family.

'We'll be back in plenty of time for lunch, Maxine,' he declared, and, having presented her with a *fait accompli*, he turned once more to Laura. 'Five minutes,' he reiterated.

Laura stared after him impotently as he went to speak to his sister. He had trapped her, and there was nothing she could do save give in with as good a grace as she could muster. Muttering dire threats under her breath, and avoiding all eyes, she spun on her heel and went to collect her purse.

Jonathan caught her as she was on her way upstairs. 'What was that all about, Laura?' he called after her, and she paused, turning to look at him over the banister.

'Quinn's taking me to church,' she explained, wilfully misunderstanding and hoping he would take the hint. He didn't.

He frowned up at her. 'I was referring to the kiss,' he said dryly.

Her throat closed over, and her skin felt prickly and uncomfortable. 'Oh, that!' She shrugged.

'Yes, that,' Jonathan agreed, and she sighed, knowing he wasn't going to let it go.

'Quinn was just making a point.'

'Which was?'

'None of your business,' she returned quietly and firmly.

'I see,' he said, and she had the uncanny feeling that he did. 'You'd better take care, then,' he advised.

She couldn't help smiling at that. 'Is that all you're going to say?'

He smiled back. 'You wouldn't listen, and you know how I hate to have my best advice ignored. Just…take care, OK?' he repeated, and strolled back into the lounge.

Wise words, she decided as she carried on up the stairs. She intended to follow them closely. It took only a couple of minutes to comb her hair, pull on a pair of warm boots and hurry downstairs again. Collecting her coat from the closet as she passed, she was shrugging it on as she went outside. Quinn already had the Bronco turned, the engine running to heat up the inside, when she climbed in beside him.

'You're late. I was beginning to think you'd chickened out,' he remarked sardonically as he put the car in motion.

She sent him a scathing look down her nose. 'I never run from bullies and cowards. Don't try your caveman tactics on me again!'

'Scared you might enjoy it and forget your rules...again?'

'That'll be the day!'

'You know, honey, every lie has to be paid for one day,' he told her without taking his eyes off the road, but she refused to rise to the bait.

After that, not surprisingly, the journey was undertaken in complete silence. They arrived at the church with scant minutes to spare. She had thought he would drop her outside, but to her surprise he came in with her. The church was full to bursting for this special service, but Quinn spoke to someone on the end of a row and everyone cheerfully squeezed up to make room for them. Then the service started, and Laura was startled to hear Quinn singing the words of a familiar carol. He had a fine voice, too. Why that should amaze her, she didn't really know. She didn't know why it should bring a strange fluttery sensation to the pit of her stomach, either.

They became separated later, when the service was over and everyone began to file out. It seemed to Laura that the entire congregation was milling around outside, greeting friends and relatives. Unable to find Quinn, she wandered to one side and propped herself against a tree to wait. As the crowd thinned, she eventually spotted him several yards away, laughing with a middle-aged couple he clearly knew well. Quinn at ease was a revelation. His smile was everything she would have expected it to be, when devoid of mockery, and the sight of it sent a curious little pain through her chest. When his laugh rang out, free and unbridled, the pain became a nagging ache.

He turned then, looking directly at her, and she realised he had known exactly where she was all the time. Like a shutter going down, she saw the laughter die out of him immediately. It had the weirdest effect on her. It was as if the sun had gone in, and she shivered. Quinn said goodbye to his friends and came to join her.

'Ready to go?' he asked coolly. Taking her agreement for granted, he started walking to where he had left the car, walking so quickly she had difficulty keeping up with his long strides.

'If you're in that much of a hurry to get me back to the house, why did you agree to bring me?' she asked crossly as she hurried along beside him.

'Because I always attend the Christmas Day service here. It was no bother to take you with me,' Quinn revealed mockingly. Reaching the Bronco, he held open the door for her to climb in. She stared at him.

'Would you care to repeat that?' she snapped irately, but that only made him smile.

'I think you heard me the first time.'

'I see,' she gritted through her teeth, and he laughed softly.

'I doubt that you do. Now, are you getting in, or do you intend to stand there all day?'

Aware that they were receiving some highly interested looks, Laura bit back her anger and climbed in. Why hadn't he told her that before, she wondered irritably, instead of letting her think he was doing her a favour? Probably because it gave him some sort of perverted pleasure. Lord, what a hateful man!

They were ten minutes into the homeward journey

when Quinn surprised her by breaking the silence which had settled around them.

'I think you should know that nobody tries to make a fool of me and gets away with it, Laura,' he declared conversationally, and she caught her breath as her nerves did a high jump.

She turned to look at him as everything suddenly fell into place. This was the real reason he had agreed to bring her. Not because he happened to be going the same way but because, out here, he was in complete control. She had nowhere to escape to; nobody to call to for help. Realising her vulnerability, Laura sat up straighter and hid her rising unease behind a show of bravado.

'I'll make a note of it in my diary as soon as we get back,' she quipped, hoping she didn't sound as nervous as she felt.

'You should hold onto that sense of humour; you might need it,' he advised, making her nerves skitter.

'Is that a threat? I thought you told me you wouldn't do anything to alarm me on the way,' she reminded him, but that only made him grin.

'Ah, but we're not on the way now, we're going home,' he pointed out mockingly, and her heart plunged at the fine distinction.

'Very clever,' she said huskily, her mouth going as dry as a desert.

'I told you you were no match for me, Laura.'

She shivered, but she was not about to reveal he had in any way unnerved her. 'OK, you've got me here. Now what?'

Quinn laughed softly. 'Now we find out if you're as cool as you say you are,' he declared, and brought the Bronco to a skidding halt on the treacherous road. They very nearly ended up nose first in the ditch. White as a ghost, Laura stared at him in horror.

'Are you crazy?' she demanded shakily. Her heart felt as if it was trying to batter its way out of her chest, and the rest of her body trembled with shock.

His smile would have done the devil proud. 'If I am, it's because you've driven me to it,' he shot back in amusement.

'You could have killed us both!'

'Doesn't it excite you to know you can make me reckless?' he taunted. Releasing both seat belts, he closed the gap between them and loomed over her. 'Now,' he said, softly menacing, 'It's time to take care of unfinished business.'

Laura had retreated instinctively, but now she was brought up short by the press of the door against her back. 'Unfinished business?' she asked unevenly, so vitally aware of his closeness that it was hard to think clearly.

'You threw down a gauntlet last night and left before I could pick it up. And I would have, because, you see, I never refuse a challenge,' he related softly, and she swallowed, licking her lips.

'I did nothing of the sort,' she denied, though she knew she had, however unintentionally.

Feral amusement danced in his eyes. 'Oh, yes, you did, sweetheart. And it wasn't just any old dare. It was a direct challenge to my manhood,' he added, and Laura's throat closed over.

'So you've decided to play the caveman to salve your wounded pride, have you?' she scorned, wondering what devious plan he had in mind. Quinn shook his head wonderingly.

'You have no sense of self-preservation, have you?'

Though she knew it probably wasn't wise to goad him, she had no other choice, for he had the upper hand. Her chin went up another notch. 'I'm not afraid of you!' she countered swiftly.

He laughed wolfishly. 'No? Your eyes are like saucers. What do you imagine I'm going to do?'

Oh, God, what a question! The truth? She imagined he would kiss her, and was afraid that he wouldn't. The wanton part of her ached for him, whilst the sensible part said she must prevent him from kissing her for her own peace of mind. If he kissed her, she would come apart in his arms, for her will-power turned to ashes when he touched her. She must not let it happen.

'Let me go,' she ordered huskily, only to see him shake his head.

He cupped her cheek with his palm and ran his thumb tantalisingly over her lips. 'I don't think so,' he told her in a gravelly voice and, when their eyes met, his were no longer cold and remote, but so hot they scorched her. 'You have the face of an angel and the soul of a black widow spider. I know it, and yet I still want to take you to my bed and sate myself with you.'

Her nerves rioted at the husky confession. Her stomach clenched as his words stoked embers which threatened to burst into flames. Could it only be days ago that she had thought it would be fun to tease this man? She wasn't laughing now. If he tried to do what he wanted, she was more likely to help him than fight him. For she was caught in the same trap. She wanted him, despite what he thought of her. It would be wonderful to let go, to lose herself in what she was beginning to believe only he could make her feel, but what then? How would she be able to live with herself afterwards?

She wouldn't be able to, and that was the truth. She had to stop this whilst she still could.

'You'll hate yourself in the morning!' she declared witheringly, but that merely made him laugh.

'I'll risk it,' he responded ironically.

Laura gritted her teeth. 'What about me?'

His brows rose. 'What about you?'

Her eyes flung angry darts at him. 'I'll fight you!'

Quinn smiled slowly. 'I'm counting on it,' he said shockingly, and she gasped in outrage.

'You're insufferable!'

'Only because I won't play the game by your rules,' he countered instantly. 'I have news for you, Laura, darling. We aren't playing by your rules any more.' Without warning his hand moved, clasping her round the back of her neck and drawing her towards him.

Alarm shot through her. Her hands lifted, pressing against his shoulders, trying to hold him off, but it had little effect. Inexorably she was drawn closer. 'What does that mean?' she demanded, panting with the effort.

'It means you are no longer in control of the field. That scares you, doesn't it, because you like to be in control? But you only have yourself to blame. You threw down the gauntlet. This is war, sweetheart, and to the victor go the spoils. I won't pay, but you will play.'

His confidence was alarming. The more so because she knew he had her own weakness on his side. Yet still she fought on, because she could not surrender. 'Never!' she denied, as her arms began to wobble, and he laughed again.

'Never say never,' he advised tauntingly.

'Never! Never! Never!' she cried, then groaned as her arms gave out and she collapsed against him.

'I did warn you,' he said softly and, pulling her onto his lap, he brought his mouth down on hers.

The touch of his lips took her breath away and, the instant her own parted, he took possession of her mouth, plundering it with a shimmering sensuality. Laura was lost before she knew it, able only to respond. They duelled, inciting each other on with a steadily mounting hunger. A moan of pleasure escaped from her throat and, as if that was what he had been waiting for, Quinn drew back, staring down into her bemused face.

'I like to hear you moan,' he declared silkily, reaching out a finger to touch her mouth.

Eyes widening in dismay as she realised what she had done, Laura jerked back. 'Let me go!' she ordered thickly, hot colour surging into her cheeks as she fought to escape his hold.

'It's too late to fight me,' he mocked, releasing her, and Laura scrambled back into her own seat.

'I don't want to fight you, I want to kill you!' she snapped witheringly, and Quinn laughed.

'Of course you do. Because you know you can't win.' he pronounced confidently, and she drew in a shaky breath.

'I know nothing of the sort,' she retorted coldly, wishing she had never agreed to this trip.

Quinn watched her thoughtfully. 'We both know you want me more than you're prepared to admit. Would you like me to prove it again?'

Laura glared at him. 'What I would like is for you to start this car and take me home,' she snapped.

'I don't blame you for being worried. You should never have crossed swords with me, Laura Maclane. I think you're going to live to regret it,' he declared prophetically, and she shivered. She regretted it already.

Quinn set the car moving once more, and Laura stared fixedly out of the window. Dear God, how had everything gone so badly wrong? She had been so sure he would be put off, but instead he had seen it as a challenge. He was going to prove that he could have her, but under his rules, not hers. It no longer mattered to him that he did not like her; he was intent on winning their private little war.

She closed her eyes. By reacting as he had, he had taken away her strongest weapons. She had relied on his dislike and disgust, and now they had been removed from the picture. The only defence she had left was her determination not to give in. She had to fight him. Not to win, but because she couldn't afford to lose.

She could not let him see she was worried. He had to believe she was as confident as ever. It was not going to be easy. She knew he was much better at this than she was. But all she had to do was hold out for the next few days. Surely she could manage that? Her jaw firmed. No doubts. She would have to. Failure was not an option. She would not become another trophy for Quinn Mannion to hang from his belt!

CHAPTER SEVEN

LAURA was surprised she enjoyed her Christmas lunch quite as much as she did. She had not expected to after what had happened on the way back from church. But Quinn had been unfailingly polite ever since, and as a consequence she had been able to relax and enjoy the friendly atmosphere which pervaded the table. Of course, she knew it was all an act on his part and that normal hostilities would resume shortly, but the respite gave her the opportunity to stiffen her resolve.

She was warmed by the way she was included in the general merriment. Admittedly, both Stella and Philip were no more than polite, but Maxine, Caroline, Jonathan and Ian made a point of making sure she did not feel left out. She was grateful for their thoughtfulness. The more so as she knew for Maxine, at least, her presence was an unhappy reminder of her husband's absence.

When the rest of the family retired to the lounge afterwards, Laura stayed behind to help Norah clear up the dirty dishes and plates of untouched food. The housekeeper protested at first but, when Laura made it clear she was not about to go away, she accepted the help gratefully.

'Don't you have family waiting for you at home, Norah?' she asked as she stacked the plates in the dishwasher.

'Course I do, miss,' the housekeeper replied, busy

123

covering dishes and stacking them in the refrigerator. 'I'll be off home as soon as I've seen to all this mess.'

Laura surveyed the amount of work to be done, and knew it would take ages. It was an unacceptable situation, and she turned to the other woman, a dirty plate in either hand. 'Oh, no, you won't. You'll go now,' she insisted, setting the plates aside and crossing to take a bowl of trifle from Norah's hands.

Norah set her hands akimbo. 'That's kind of you, but it's my place to see everything is cleared up, she said stiffly, but behind the proud front Laura could clearly see she wanted to go, but was not sure she should.

'I'll tell Mrs Harrington I told you to go,' Laura added, and the housekeeper frowned doubtfully.

'I don't know...'

'Well, I do. This is Christmas, Norah. You should be with your family, not here waiting on us. Go!' Laura ordered with a smile.

Smiling suddenly, Norah whipped off her apron, folded it neatly, and placed it over the back of a chair. 'There's plenty of food in the pantry for supper, if anyone's hungry,' she said as she collected her coat from a hook and slipped it on.

Laura saw her to the door. 'We won't starve. Now you forget all about us and go and enjoy yourself. Merry Christmas, Norah,' she called out as she waved the other woman goodbye.

Satisfied she had done the right thing, Laura turned to survey the room, and grimaced. There wasn't a spare inch of surface anywhere. The food was the important thing, though, and she set to with a will, putting everything away so it would keep for later. She was in the process of trying to find room for one last dish in the refrigerator when Quinn walked in.

His eyebrows shot up when he saw her. 'Where's Norah?'

Laura looked round with a start and nearly dropped the plate. Quinn reached out and steadied it, and they ended up face to face.

'I sent her home. I'm sorry if that annoys you, but she should be with her family,' she told him shortly, chin raised for argument, but Quinn merely nodded.

'I was coming to do the same thing. Do you need any help?'

She wasn't quite flabbergasted, but he had certainly taken the wind out of her sails. However, she was not one to look a gift horse in the mouth. She handed him the plate.

'See if you can find a place for that whilst I finish loading the dishwasher.'

She heard him swear once or twice as she filled the drawers, and grinned to herself.

'Anything else?' he asked suddenly from right behind her, and she jumped out of her skin, dropping a glass and watching in horror as it smashed on the floor.

'You're hell on glasses,' Quinn murmured dryly, bringing stinging colour to her cheeks.

'It was an accident!' she exclaimed, squatting down to pick up the pieces.

'Leave it!' he ordered instantly, but it was too late; she felt a stinging in her palm and gasped at the sudden pain. 'Of all the idiots...!' Quinn declared witheringly, catching her by the wrist and pulling her to her feet. 'Here, let me see.'

'It's just a scratch,' Laura said faintly. It wasn't the sight of her own blood which turned her knees weak, but the touch of his hand on hers. She found herself studying the top of his head, and the urge to run her fingers through his hair was incredibly strong. She groaned, ordering herself to get a grip, and he glanced up sharply.

'What's wrong?' he demanded, and she flushed as she realised he had heard her.

'It smarts,' she fabricated hastily, and he gave her a look.

'Don't be such a baby!' he snorted, and held her hand over the sink whilst he ran the cold water. Laura bit her lip as the icy water cleaned the small cut.

'It looks clean,' Quinn pronounced with satisfaction, drying her off with a kitchen towel. 'Didn't you ever learn not to touch broken glass?'

Laura pursed her lips, wishing he would simply let her go. 'Apparently not,' she retorted, following like a recalcitrant lamb as he took her to where the first-aid box was kept and proceeded to cover the cut with a Band-Aid. 'Thank you,' she said grudgingly, and he cast her a quizzical look.

'Are you always this ungrateful?'

'Only when someone makes that much fuss!' she snapped back, and he shook his head, smiling wryly.

'It must be lack of food,' he remarked, producing a dustpan from a cupboard and squatting to sweep up the mess.

'Excuse me?'

He straightened, disposing of the shards in a box he found in the trash. 'Your short temper. At lunch you barely ate anything. You seemed more intent on making a still life out of your food,' Quinn observed dryly, and she frowned, realising he must have been watching her, and not liking it.

'I wasn't very hungry,' she excused herself.

'Was it something I said?' he asked in amusement,

and she had no trouble knowing he was referring to what had happened earlier. She sent him a withering look.

'I doubt very much that anything you said would have an effect on me, Quinn,' she responded frostily.

'Darling,' he interjected, and her nerves jolted.

'What?'

'You forgot to say darling,' he prompted silkily.

Something lodged itself in her throat, and she had the devil of a job to speak round it. 'Did I?' she asked scratchily, and he smiled.

'Don't you love me any more, Laura, darling?' he taunted softly, and her heart skipped wildly at the novel idea of loving Quinn Mannion.

'Do you want me to love you, Quinn, *darling?*' she retorted, whilst her mouth went dry and the bottom seemed to fall out of her stomach. She had no idea why she was reacting so violently to a joke. She didn't love him. She couldn't.

He laughed dryly. 'I don't think I would survive your kind of love.'

She smiled back. 'Then it's as well neither of us loves the other, isn't it?' she declared, holding his gaze.

His eyes darkened. 'On the other hand, I would love to have you, and you would love to have me,' he said in a silky undertone, just as the door flew open and Tom barrelled in, followed more circumspectly by his mother and sister, and Jonathan.

'For goodness' sake, you two aren't still at logger-heads, are you?' Caroline exclaimed disgustedly, and her brother sent her a devilish grin.

'Actually, we were merely discussing the possibility of you and Jonathan naming the day,' Quinn retorted, and both his sister and his friend went red.

'Quinn!' Caroline exclaimed in embarrassment, pressing her hands to her hot cheeks.

'Well, you do mean to marry him, don't you?' he teased her affectionately, and she groaned.

'For goodness' sake, he hasn't asked me!' she protested faintly.

'An oversight, I'm sure,' her brother declared, looking pointedly at Jonathan, who returned the look squarely.

'You know, I'd call you out if it was still in fashion!' he remarked calmly.

'You could try punching me on the nose,' Quinn responded with a grin.

Jonathan laughed. 'I'd do more than try, my friend.'

'And my sister?'

'Mind your own business.'

Quinn spread his hands. 'You see, I told you he loves you,' he said, and Caroline groaned and started to laugh.

'If I didn't love you so much, I'd kill you for what you just did. Just behave yourself for five minutes. We came out to ask you if you wanted to help us build a snowman.'

'Laura, too,' Ellie piped up, swinging on her mother's hand and looking up at Laura solemnly.

Quinn glanced at Laura with a decided glint in his eye. 'Oh, I think Laura would prefer to remain inside in the warm,' he remarked goadingly. 'She might break a nail.'

She sent him a look designed to inflict a fatal wound. 'I'll have you know I'm the world's best snowman maker!' she exclaimed, and Tom giggled. She winked at him.

'This I have to see,' Quinn taunted.

'You will. Just give me a few minutes to change my clothes and I'll be right with you.'

Fired up by the need to put him in his place, she ran upstairs to put on something warmer. She would show the arrogant devil what a Maclane could do.

It was wonderful outside. The air was crisp and fresh, and the six of them worked like beavers to build a huge snowman. Soon the four adults were laughing like kids, getting in each other's way and generally fooling around. Cheeks grew rosy, and each breath misted before their eyes. Laura was glad of her woollen hat and gloves which kept her cosy and warm.

An hour later, the result of their efforts stood proudly beside the drive. It had a carrot for its nose, purloined from the kitchen for the purpose, stones for eyes, and an old pipe stuck in where its mouth should be. An old cloth cap sat at a rakish angle on its head and a scarf lay looped around its neck. The children loved it, declaring it the best snowman ever.

Who threw the first snowball wasn't clear, but pretty soon everyone was throwing them. Shrieks and laughter bubbled out. Laura soon found herself covered with snow. Darting round a corner of the house, she took a second to catch her breath and made a small pile of snowballs ready to throw. Peeping round the corner, she sought a target. She had a good eye and a good arm, and her missile caught Jonathan on the back of the head.

He turned with a roar, but she had dodged back out of sight. Collecting several balls, she stepped round the corner. Quinn squatted down mere yards away. Her first ball caught him on the ear, the second full in the face as he turned round to find the culprit. He saw her standing there laughing at him and rose to his feet menacingly. With a squeal, Laura turned and ran down the side of the house and round the back.

Feet pounded behind her and something hit her with

a solid thwack in the middle of her back. Laughing and gasping for breath, she tracked across what was the lawn in summer and dodged in between two rhododendron bushes. Feverishly she pounded snow into balls as if her life depended on it and, taking one in each hand, peered round the bush. To her surprise, there wasn't a soul in sight.

'Hey!' a voice called from behind her, and she spun round.

A large soft ball of snow hit her in the face, finding its way into her nose and mouth. She staggered, shaking her head like a dog, and was caught by two more missiles before she could move. Wiping her eyes, she saw Quinn's dark shape advancing on her and launched her own ammunition, but he dodged them easily. She turned to run then but he dived after her, catching her foot and bringing her down into a deep drift of snow. Laughing, she tried to crawl away but he was on her in a second, turning her over to straddle her hips. She managed to grab a handful of snow and force it down his neck before he caught her arms and pinioned them beside her head.

Laughing, breathing as if they had run a marathon, they stared at each other.

'Where'd you learn to throw like that?' Quinn gasped, grimacing as melted snow trickled down inside his shirt.

Laura licked snow off her lips as she tried to catch her breath. 'I used to play baseball with the other kids on the block. I was their star pitcher.' Until some of the boys started complaining about being struck out by a girl. It was an unfair world.

Quinn settled himself against her more comfortably. The effect was instantly arousing, and her breath caught in her throat as she felt the warmth of his legs cradling her hips. She went utterly still, no longer laughing. She realised then that she had forgotten to be cautious and could only watch helplessly as his eyes roved over her at their leisure, taking in the damp tendrils of hair which clung to her rosy cheeks, her coat which rose and fell rapidly with every breath she took, down to her jean-clad hips resting between his legs. When his eyes met hers again, they held a gleam which set all her nerves rocking.

'What's the matter, Laura?' he taunted softly.

'Nothing,' she denied breathlessly, kicking herself for her mistake.

One lazy eyebrow shot up. 'Nothing? Are you sure? You seem a little…tensed up to me.'

To her chagrin she felt betraying colour enter her cheeks. 'It's cold.'

His lips curved. 'Really? I'd have said you were getting a little overheated myself.'

Laura ground her teeth together. The rat was enjoying this. He knew exactly what he was doing to her, and he was determined to get his pound of flesh. She glared at him but said nothing.

'Why don't you tell me to let you go?' he suggested huskily, and though she wanted to remain silent she had to get him off her before she did something stupid. Like reach up and pull him down to her.

'L-let me go,' she complied, but her voice was barely more than a croak.

Blue eyes scorched her as he tutted. 'You'll have to say it like you mean it,' he mocked, lowering his head to within a breath of hers. 'That sounded more like you were begging me to make love to you.'

'Never!' she denied as his head lowered that final inch. At the very last second she turned her head away, so that his lips found the tender skin of her neck. 'Don't!'

His lips burned her. 'Liar. Tell me what you really want me to do.'

'Nothing. I want you to do nothing,' she whispered painfully, and felt his hands leave her wrists to cup her face and turn her towards him.

'I don't believe you.'

'You never have.'

He laughed as he stared deeply into her eyes. 'Would it help if I told you you're the most beautiful woman I've ever seen? That no other woman has ever done this to me? It's true, you know. I should be shivering with the cold, but all I can think of is burying myself deep inside you, and hearing you cry out in pleasure,' he told her shockingly. Only she wasn't so much shocked as excited. Desire kicked deep inside her, starting up an unrelenting, throbbing ache.

Laura closed her eyes, desperately trying to shut out the pictures he evoked, but it was impossible. 'Stop it,' she ordered scratchily, and he raised his head to look down at her once more.

'You don't really mean that. We both know it. It is going to happen. I am going to make love to you. Only, like I told you, I won't be paying for it. You're going to ask me,' he declared.

Laura swallowed a lump which threatened to choke her. 'Never in this lifetime!' she denied as strongly as she could, and with a laugh Quinn rolled off her and stood up.

'Oh, yes, Laura, darling. In this lifetime, and probably more than once. With you, once would never be enough,' he taunted, bending down and pulling her to her feet.

'You'd better get out of those wet clothes. We don't want you to catch a chill,' he advised sardonically. 'Do you need any help?'

How she kept from hitting him, she didn't know. 'Why don't you—?' She never finished the sentence, for Quinn reached out and placed a hand over her mouth.

'Careful, Laura, your temper is showing,' he warned, and she glared at him for a second or two before turning on her heel and walking away to the sound of his soft laughter.

Damn him, she cursed as she skirted the bushes and set off back across the lawn. He was cutting through her defences like a hot knife through butter, making her pay for that stupid challenge she had laid down. She had bargained on him being too proud a man to pay, but not on him turning the tables on her, using her undeniable attraction to him against her.

He was wrong about her reasons for wanting to keep him at bay. It had nothing to do with control, and everything to do with the fact that she would not be able to live with herself if she slept with a man she knew did not like her. Yet she longed to know what it would be like to be made love to by him. And the truth was, if she stayed here, she would probably find out. Every time he touched her, it became harder and harder to push him away.

God, what kind of woman did that make her? How could she want a man who was determined to have her, just to prove he could? Because she was a fool. Because only a fool would have allowed herself to fall in love with him in the first place!

The statement popped into her mind from out of no-where, staggering her, taking her breath away. She reached out for the wall, leaning against it for support as she probed the truth of it. Was it really possible she had fallen in love with Quinn and not known it? Was that what this despairing feeling inside her was all about? Did she *love* Quinn Mannion?

Laura searched her heart and groaned at the truth she found emblazoned there. It was true. She had looked into his eyes that first time, and fallen headlong. His attitude to her had hidden the truth. She had been so angry with him, she hadn't seen what was right there in front of her eyes. She saw it now, though, and there was no joy in the knowledge. For, though she might know now what had happened to her, it didn't change how Quinn felt. He most certainly did not love her. He wanted her, but love had nothing to do with it.

Laura closed her eyes. She knew what she had to do. She had to leave. She could not stay here and risk that he might discover her secret. That must not be allowed to happen. She could not bear him knowing. Not now. Not when she felt so raw. Lord, how he would laugh if he knew what she had done!

With another groan she pushed herself away from the wall. By leaving she would be forfeiting any chance she had of telling Maxine Harrington the truth any time soon, but there was no other way. She was too vulnerable, too open to hurt such as she had never known before. She would make other plans when her mind was clearer.

She rounded the house, and there were Caroline, Jonathan and the two children, playing as if nothing had happened. A sob escaped her tight throat. Nothing had happened to them. She was the one whose whole world had just crashed down around her hapless head.

CHAPTER EIGHT

LAURA was exhausted by the time she let herself into her apartment. It had been a particularly busy day at the studio. Her partner, Anya, had gone down with the flu, and she had been trying to cover both of their current commissions by herself for the last few days. All she needed was for Felix, their invaluable assistant, to succumb to the bug, and it would really make her week.

Dumping her bag on her bed, she shrugged off her coat and tossed it aside, too weary to be neat right now. Kicking off her shoes, she padded into her compact kitchen and boiled water for some herb tea. When it was ready, she took her mug into the lounge and collapsed onto the couch, tucking her feet up under her.

She wondered if she could persuade Jonathan to stay home tonight. They were supposed to be attending a charity function, but she was scarcely in the mood. She hadn't, she admitted honestly, been in the mood for some time. Three weeks to be precise.

It was three weeks since Christmas. Three endless weeks since she had discovered she had made the monumental error of falling hopelessly in love with Quinn Mannion. After she had made the decision to leave, she hadn't delayed acting upon it. She had left the very next day without ever having seen Quinn again.

She had been working flat out ever since. Trying to work him out of her system. She had virtually haunted the studio, intent on making herself so tired she was scarcely thinking about him more than a dozen times an hour. It ought to have worked. It didn't surprise her that it failed. Just when she thought she was succeeding, he would pop into her mind and, instead of working on a colour scheme, she would sit at her desk, her thoughts a hundred miles away on a man who had probably never given her another thought! It was crazy. If only she could forget how it felt to be held by him. If only she hadn't been so foolish as to fall in love with him!

Laura set her mug aside with a groan. How she hated feeling this way. Loathed herself for her inability to put Quinn from her mind. Each moment she had spent with him replayed itself with crystal clarity. It was torture, but she wasn't able to stop it. She had the dreadful feeling that she would never forget Quinn as long as she lived.

A glance at her watch told her it was late. She would have to start getting ready. Putting her reluctance aside, Laura went to take a shower and change into the cocktail dress she had bought for the occasion. Cut straight, the dress was made of emerald-green taffeta. Thin shoulder straps held up a bodice covered with a delicate tracery of silver threadwork.

She looked good in it, and that boosted her spirits so that by the time she had put on discreet make-up, fastened diamond studs in her ears and draped a gold locket inset with semiprecious stones about her throat she was almost looking forward to the evening.

The doorbell rang as she finished dabbing perfume on her pulse spots. As ready as she was ever likely to be, Laura set the bottle down and went to answer its summons. She threw open the door with a smile, and felt it fade on her lips.

Standing outside, looking stunningly handsome in his white dinner jacket and black bow tie, was Quinn. It seemed to Laura, who suddenly needed to hold onto the door for support, that as if by thinking about him she had somehow conjured him up.

'Hello, Laura,' he greeted her in his slightly husky voice, setting her senses leaping wildly.

The shock was enormous, the pleasure immense. She had not known until that very second the depth of pleasure just looking at him could give her. Her heart twisted painfully. She had missed him. It was as if a missing part of her had suddenly fallen into place. God help her, he was her destiny. The other half which made her whole. There should have been joy in the knowledge, but all it did was sharpen the pain. What cruel twist of fate was it which brought him to her door?

'What are you doing here, Quinn?' she asked bluntly. She had had no idea he even knew where she lived.

Quinn slipped his hands into his trouser pockets, observing her silently for a moment. He looked supremely male, stirring her as no other man could. It irked her that he could appear so relaxed, when her own nerves were skittering like crazy at his unexpected appearance.

'Aren't you going to invite me in?' he asked, one eyebrow raised mockingly.

She didn't want to. She knew that if she let him in his presence would be forever imprinted on the apartment. 'I'm expecting Jonathan,' she replied shortly, her heart thumping so loudly she was surprised he couldn't hear it.

'Jonathan is going straight to the hotel. He sent me to collect you.'

Her body rocked with the shock. 'Sent you?' she challenged. Jonathan wouldn't have done this to her. He was her friend.

Quinn glanced pointedly to his left. 'I'll explain where

the rest of the world can't listen in,' he said ironically, and, popping her head out, Laura saw one of her neighbours hovering in a doorway a little way down the hall.

She bit her lip. Emily Collins was a dear old thing, but a dreadful gossip too. Tomorrow it would be all over the building that she had had 'a gentleman caller'. With reluctance she stepped back. 'You'd better come in, then,' she invited grudgingly.

'Thank you,' Quinn murmured dryly and, with a nod to the old lady which put her in quite a dither, stepped into the apartment.

Laura closed the door and followed him into the lounge. The room had always seemed spacious before, but his presence dwarfed it. He stood in the centre of the floor and looked around.

'Is this all Alex could afford?' he asked coolly, and she caught her breath angrily at the implication that her home had been some kind of love-nest.

'Alexander didn't buy this place, I did,' she told him shortly, folding her arms and running her palms over tingling skin.

'I expected something more...'

'Trashy? I'm sorry to disappoint you.'

He looked at her in amusement. 'I was going to say up-market. Something more elegant and sterile. This is much more homey. I'm surprised.'

Laura wasn't entirely sure if that was a compliment or not, and chose not to pursue the matter. 'You were going to tell me about Jonathan,' she reminded him baldly.

'Ah, yes. I have tickets to the same function, and I managed to convince Caroline to come with me. When I realised Jonathan was bringing you, I suggested we swap partners. He was only too happy to agree. He said he knew you would understand.'

Her heart sank. Of course she understood why he had chosen to throw her to the wolf. He loved Caroline and naturally he would want to be with her. He would have no way of knowing how unwelcome the change of partners would be to her, because she had told him nothing of her feelings for Quinn. Under the circumstances, the alternative scenario was not acceptable. She would be a fool to give herself more grief.

'Well, that's all very fine and dandy, but I have no intention of going anywhere with you,' she returned with all the cool at her command. Spending any time with Quinn would be a mistake. She couldn't afford to make that kind of fatal error.

Quinn sighed, running a ruminative finger along the ridge of his nose. 'I thought that would be your answer. It raises a problem. If you don't go, Caroline won't go.'

Her hand rose to her throat where her pulse beat jerkily. 'You're making that up!' she accused.

'I wish I were. She was quite adamant about it. You have to be there too.'

Laura bit her lip in dismay. She didn't understand why Caroline should insist on her presence. It made no sense. She had to know Laura and her brother didn't get along.

'This is crazy. I didn't even want to go to the damn function in the first place! Why did you have to suggest it?'

'Because I want my sister to be happy,' Quinn replied simply. 'Look at it this way. You might have to spend a few uncomfortable hours, but for Jonathan and my sister it will be heaven.'

Damn, but he was clever. Put that way, how could she refuse? It would be churlish.

'All right, you win. I just hope they appreciate what I'm about to do,' she said wryly, accepting the inevitable with as much grace as she could muster.

'I'm sure they will,' Quinn said dryly. 'If you're ready, we can go.'

Laura shivered. She knew this was a mistake, but it was beyond her power to change anything. 'I won't be a moment.' She excused herself and retreated to her bedroom.

Shutting the door behind her, she closed her eyes and sank back against it. Instead of shutting Quinn out, it gave her a vivid mental picture of him. He looked so damned sexy in his dinner suit. It fitted him to perfection, outlining a body her hands quite literally itched to explore.

In her chest, her heart was racing madly and she pressed a trembling hand over it. Why had this had to happen now? She didn't need this! Oh, but how alive she suddenly felt! Her hands lifted to burning cheeks. It was so unfair!

Fair or not, she couldn't remain in her bedroom much longer. She had to make the best of it. Taking a deep breath, Laura ran her fingers over her hair, smoothing it down as if the act could soothe her shattered calm. There was nothing to do save get through the evening as best she could.

Grabbing up her coat and purse, she rejoined Quinn in the lounge. He was standing at the window, so deep in thought he hadn't heard her return. Her heart lurched. What was it about him that made all other men pale by comparison? She had never been this attuned to anyone. It was unnerving. *He* was unnerving. He only had to look at her and she melted. It was as if he had cast a spell over her. Which was all very well in a fairy tale, but this was for real, and not nearly so amusing.

'I'm ready,' she announced coolly, and he turned, his eyes running over her, setting a tide of warmth ebbing and flowing within her.

Quinn came forward and took her coat, holding it out for her to slip her arms into the sleeves. 'Did I tell you how beautiful you look tonight?' he murmured as he draped the fabric over her shoulders, bringing her close enough to smell the tantalising aroma of his cologne.

Laura drew in a ragged breath. Lord, he was so close it would be easy to lean back against him and forget everything. Which would be the height of insanity. Stiffening her spine, she took a step away from him.

'Don't waste your efforts, Quinn. I've already agreed to go,' she drawled with heavy irony.

'Why is it so hard to accept a compliment from me?' he asked sardonically, and she steeled herself to face him.

It was like drowning to look into the blue depths of his eyes. It would be so easy to lose herself in him. He drew her like no other man, and she knew it would never be like this with anyone else. It was enough to break her heart.

'Because you dislike me. Or are you going to tell me you've had a miraculous conversion and are now madly in love with me?' she scoffed, even as a tiny part of her foolish heart couldn't help but hope he would say yes. She should have known better. Quinn Mannion was not the kind to change his mind once it was made up, and he had made up his mind about her a very long time ago.

'That's as unlikely as you declaring you love me. Love has nothing to do with our relationship. We want each other, but that's all,' he informed her, going past her to open the front door. 'Shall we go? I have a taxi waiting downstairs.'

It shouldn't have hurt to hear what she already knew but, of course, it did. Because she loved him, he now had a thousand ways to hurt her.

She kept a good distance between them in the elevator, a fact he noted with patent amusement. However, the taxi was a different proposition. It was impossible not to be vitally aware of him. She tried to keep herself to the side, but the driver took corners as if he were practising for the Indy 500 and, no matter what she did, she kept bumping into Quinn. She lost her breath every time their thighs brushed, and once very nearly landed in his lap and he had to lend a hand to push her upright.

'Sorry,' she said.

His eyes gleamed back at her. 'I'm not. I have fantasies about you sitting on my lap,' he returned outrageously, and Laura shot him a fulminating look, painfully aware of the driver listening to everything they said.

'For heaven's sake!' she protested, grabbing at the door as they made a wild right turn.

'Come over here, then you won't be shaken about so much,' he invited drolly, and Laura wanted very much to hit him. He knew as well as she did that if she did she might not shake but she would most certainly tremble.

'I'm happier right here,' she refused, and heard rather than saw him shrug.

'Safety is a relative thing, darling,' he remarked, and she frowned.

'What is that supposed to mean?'

'It means you think you're safe, but you're only as safe as I want you to be. Why did you run away?'

The question, tacked onto the end of an already alarming statement, tied her stomach in knots.

'I didn't run away,' she denied instantly, and of course he didn't believe her.

'It was a rash thing to do,' he went on as if she hadn't spoken. 'It only underlined what I already knew.'

Laura knew it was probably fatal to respond, but she couldn't let it pass either. 'And what is that?'

'That you're going to end up in bed with me very soon,' he told her confidently, and Laura felt her heart sink. She had thought, hoped, his intentions would have been abandoned when she left the house, but she knew now she was wrong. He felt as strongly as he always had, and she would do well to remember it.

'Only in your dreams!' she shot back smartly.

Quinn laughed softly. 'In my dreams we've already made love. Reality is going to be much better,' he added provocatively.

She glared at him in the shadowed interior. 'I'm not going to bed with you, Quinn!' she declared forcefully. 'Not now. Not ever.'

'We'll see,' he said smoothly, and she pressed her lips together tightly to prevent herself from saying anything more. It would have been pointless anyway. He wasn't listening.

She was inordinately glad when they arrived at their destination only a few minutes later, and she could get out of the claustrophobic atmosphere of the taxi. Inside the hotel, she took as long as she dared in the cloakroom, but eventually she had to rejoin Quinn. He had procured drinks in her absence, and handed her a glass of white wine.

'Have you seen Jonathan?' she asked, taking a sip of the cold liquid. She wondered if she dared drain the glass. She could do with a bracer. But on an empty stomach all it was likely to do was go to her head. Tonight she needed her wits about her.

'Not yet. Let's circulate,' he suggested, cupping her elbow and steering her into the crowd.

The touch of his fingers on her bare flesh was like a brand. She tried to shake him off, but he refused to release her. Left with only the option of making an undignified scene, she was forced to concede him the small victory.

'Do you know any of these people?' she asked in an attempt to distract herself.

'Not as many as think they know me,' he responded dryly, and she laughed.

'Every silver lining has a cloud, hmm?' she returned waspishly, then caught sight of a portly gentleman who was bearing down on them at a rate of knots. 'Do you know him?' she asked sweetly, and Quinn groaned.

'Hell!' he exclaimed in a hunted undertone, and cast about him for a means of escape. 'This way,' he declared, dragging her after him as he plunged into the crowd.

They ended up in the seclusion of a window embrasure somewhere near the other end of the room. Watching Quinn peer round the drapes, Laura burst out laughing.

'Do you owe him money or something?' she teased, and he grinned ruefully.

'Very funny. The man calls himself my biggest fan. I can't go anywhere without him turning up.'

Her grey eyes danced. 'You should be flattered.'

'I was until he kept me cornered for almost an hour

once, discussing the motivations of my characters. I tell you, water torture has nothing on this man!'

'Poor Quinn,' she giggled.

'I'm overwhelmed by your sympathy,' he responded wryly, leaning a shoulder against the wall and eyeing her with reluctant amusement. 'You should laugh more often.'

'So should you,' Laura rejoined huskily.

They smiled at each other in one of those rare moments of complete understanding. Just for a second they were two people without a history. They could have been there together because they wanted to be, enjoying an evening with the person they most wanted to be with.

Which, of course, was closer to the truth for her than she cared to think about. She glanced away quickly, lest she somehow reveal her true feelings. The only thing that made being with him partway bearable was knowing he didn't know she loved him.

'Do you attend many of these functions?' she asked, with a casualness she was far from feeling.

Quinn sipped at his drink. 'One or two. I prefer to donate anonymously.'

'You're not impressed by the open display of generosity?'

'Not when I know many of these people turn out only because it would be bad for their image not to be seen doing so,' he enlarged sardonically, and she had to look at him then.

'That's a rather sweeping statement. There must be some here with truly philanthropic intentions,' she argued.

'Of course,' Quinn acknowledged, 'but they rather get lost in the crowd. It's almost obscene that people come to a function in aid of charity dripping with diamonds.'

'True, but if they weren't allowed to show off they wouldn't come, and wouldn't give their much needed money,' she pointed out. 'It's a necessary trade-off.'

'And trade-offs are something you know a great deal about, don't you?' he returned softly, taking her by surprise.

The barb reached its target with dismaying accuracy, and it felt to Laura as if he had slapped her. She drew in a shaken breath, wondering how much of that she could take before he tore her heart to shreds.

Still, she managed a frosty smile. 'It's a wonder you want anything to do with me, thinking the way you do!' she shot back, and he grinned roguishly.

'If I was thinking with my head, I wouldn't,' he confessed, eyes dropping to her throat. 'Did Alex give you that locket?'

Automatically her hand went to her throat, fingering the inlaid locket. She caressed it gently with her fingers.

'No. What made you think that?' she queried, and he pushed himself away from the wall, frowning down at what she had always thought a simple piece of jewellery.

'Because they are very fine stones. It would have been very expensive,' he revealed calmly, and Laura laughed dismissively.

'Don't be silly. It can't have. This was left to me by my mother. It was a present to her from my father.'

'If I were you, I would get it valued and insured,' Quinn advised, leaving Laura feeling rather dazed.

'Are you sure? I had no idea of its value.' She wore it because it was the only object which linked her parents together. It held the pictures of her mother and Alexander which had been taken before she was born.

'They're both dead?' Quinn asked, watching her with a strange expression on his face.

Laura felt a lump of emotion rise to her throat. 'Yes,' she confirmed, her fingers absently tightening on the locket.

'You miss them?'

She sighed. 'Very much. Of course, I scarcely knew my father. We...didn't have very long together.'

'It's unfortunate when a child loses a parent,' he remarked, and Laura didn't try to correct his assumption.

'Do Tom and Ellie remember their father?' she asked instead.

'Tom does. Ellie was just a baby at the time.'

'There's no logic in it. Why do the good have to die young?'

'Because God has other work for them to do,' Quinn said softly, and she sent him a startled look because it was not the sort of thing she expected him to say.

'Do you believe that?'

He shrugged. 'I'm not sure, but it's a comforting thought.'

He was right, it was. 'You're a strange man, Quinn Mannion,' she declared with a wry shake of her head.

'My mother loves me,' he responded wryly, and her heart turned over, for she loved him too.

'Only your mother could love you!' she retorted smartly, finishing her drink and setting her glass aside. 'Your fan must be gone by now. We ought to look for Jonathan and your sister. They'll be wondering where we are,' she said, stepping out into the mêlée. She had taken no more than half a dozen steps when his hand slipped into the crook of her arm.

'You don't think a woman could love me, Laura?'

Oh, God! What a question to ask her of all people! 'Not if they had any sense,' she countered.

'I would be quite a catch,' he pointed out.

He would indeed. Especially if he happened to love her back, Laura agreed silently. 'If they could catch you!' she said dryly. 'Besides, you're not interested in just one woman.'

'I'm only interested in one right now,' he reminded her huskily, and every nerve in her body quivered.

'You're wasting your time.'

'Like I said. We'll see.'

What he would see, Laura thought grimly, was that he had made a big mistake.

It took them almost ten minutes to find Jonathan and Caroline, for the function rooms were bursting at the seams.

'Where on earth have you been?' Caroline demanded of her brother when they finally arrived at the table Jonathan had secured.

'Avoiding Quinn's fan club,' Laura put in mockingly, and he pushed in the chair he had been holding for her just enough so that she sat down with a bump. 'Hey!'

'Sorry.' Quinn apologised with patent insincerity. 'Excuse me a moment. There's someone over there I have to speak to,' he declared, and took himself off before she could retaliate.

'Oh, dear,' Caroline sighed. 'You're still fighting, then?'

'Only to the death,' Laura retorted with a wry laugh, then relented and smiled at the other woman. 'How are you, Caroline? Who's looking after the children?'

'I'm fine. The children are with my husband's parents for the night. They adore babysitting—heaven knows why!' she added with a laugh.

'That's easy. After one night, they get to give them back again,' Jonathan answered drolly. 'Caro, you don't mind if I dance with Laura, do you?' he said a moment later, and Caroline shook her head instantly.

'Off you go. Just don't let him tread on your toes!' She waved them off with her blessing and a warning which made Laura laugh.

'Forgiven me for wishing Quinn on you?' he asked as they slowly circled the floor.

'I'm thinking about it,' she responded with a faint smile. 'Why did Caroline want me here?'

'Caro? Sorry, Laura, you've lost me there,' Jonathan replied, mystified, and Laura frowned.

'Quinn said—' she began, only to break off with a gasp.

'Quinn said what?' he prompted, but she shook her head, too furious to speak.

He had tricked her. He had known she would refuse to come here with him, and he had used his sister against her because he knew she had a soft spot for her.

'Damn him!' she swore softly, and Jonathan chuckled.

'I take it Quinn has been less than honest about something,' he drawled, and Laura sighed.

'If I get through tonight without murdering him, it will be a miracle,' she said dryly.

'In that case, if you need a good lawyer, you know where to find me,' Jonathan said tongue-in-cheek.

'Time to change partners,' Quinn suggested in a cool tone from right beside her, and Laura's head shot round to meet an inimitable gaze. He didn't allow her to refuse but released his sister and took Laura's hand, leaving Jonathan no other option but to release her and turn to Caroline. As Quinn swept her away, she saw him watching them curiously.

'Would you care to explain just how much your sister wanted me here?' she demanded of him once he had put the width of the room between them and the other couple.

'I lied,' he answered unrepentantly, and anger bubbled up inside her.

'Why?'

Quinn glanced down at her, his lips curling mockingly. 'Can't you guess? Because I wanted you here.'

'And you always get what you want?'

'Always. Remember that. Now shut that delicious mouth of yours before I shut it for you, and dance,' he commanded, pulling her against him and anchoring her there with an arm around her back.

Laura stifled a moan. She wanted to struggle, but he was holding her too tightly. Their bodies were moulded together as he moved them to the music. She tried to remain aloof by holding herself rigid, but Quinn had other ideas. His hand began a slow caress up and down her back, bringing every nerve-end to life. She knew it would be dangerous to give in, but every glide of his palm was draining the will to fight out of her so that, in the end, with a muffled sigh, she relaxed against him. Then, of course, it was too late. She didn't want to move. It felt too good. She wanted to stay right where she was, experiencing the soft seduction of his touch.

Caught, she rested her head against his shoulder and let herself drift. Lord, he felt so strong, so...safe. It was a curious sensation, when she knew he was dangerous. But she could hear his heart thudding in time with her own, and it was so easy to let her eyes close. The moment she did, her other senses leapt to the fore. She was vitally aware of every brush of his thigh between hers as they slowly moved to the music. He made no effort to hide his state of arousal and it stirred her, starting up an ache of longing deep within her. Her breasts quickened, feeling so tender, their nipples tight buds that she wanted to press against him to find relief.

In the recesses of her mind she knew she should never have touched him, but it was too late now. Being close to him turned her insides molten and her legs to jelly. To remain was to ask for trouble, yet she could no more walk away than she could swim the ocean.

'Feels good, doesn't it?' she heard Quinn murmur just above her ear, and the brush of his breath made her shiver. 'But it could be better. Much, much better.'

Laura's heart took a frantic leap. She knew he was referring to how it would be when they made love. The slip struck her. When had she started accepting the inevitable? She would not go to bed with him, however much he tempted her. Her heart would never survive it.

'A month or so ago you were nothing more than a name on a legal document, and now...' He let the sentence hang between them.

Now he was a man who had turned her world upside down, so that her life would never be the same again.

She raised her head, steeling herself to meet his eyes. 'This isn't going to work.'

Quinn laughed softly. 'Now we're two people who want each other so badly, it's driving us out of our minds.'

The truth of that made her stomach kick on a powerful wave of desire. There was no point in denying how much she wanted him. He knew. He had always known.

'Come to bed with me, Laura,' he murmured temptingly.

Her hand balled into a fist on his shoulder. 'No,' she refused, finding it painfully hard to say when he held her so closely and she wanted him so much.

'You know you want to,' Quinn urged, sultry blue eyes boring into hers.

Lord, how she did want to. It would be the most wonderful experience, but she couldn't do it. Her throat closed over, but she didn't take her gaze away from his. 'No.'

'Laura, Laura, we could be so good together, if only you'd let us. Don't tell me you haven't thought about how it would be between us.'

It sometimes seemed as if she thought of nothing else. 'The answer is still no,' she persisted valiantly, and was inordinately relieved when the music came to an end at that moment.

'Saved by the bell!' Quinn exclaimed sardonically.

He released her and took her arm to steer her back to their table. They didn't dance again, which was a relief to Laura. Once was more than enough. That kind of pleasure was as close to pain as she cared to go.

For the next hour she made a fairly good pretence of enjoying herself, but there wasn't a minute that went by when she wasn't vitally aware of Quinn. He had been in a strange mood ever since they had sat down. His eyes when they fell on her, which was often, were brooding. He became quieter, too, as the evening progressed, scarcely addressing more than a handful of words to her. She sensed a growing impatience inside him, which she found extremely unsettling. Quinn was usually so cool and in control. This wasn't like him at all.

Then Jonathan took Caroline onto the dance floor once more, and no sooner had they disappeared from view than Quinn got to his feet.

'Let's go,' he said decisively, and she frowned. It wasn't her plan to go anywhere with him.

'Go where?'

'I'm taking you home,' he told her, and she let out a ragged sigh of relief. Home was where she wanted to be, too.

'What about the others?' she pointed out even as she stood up and collected her purse.

Quinn left a note, written on the back of an invitation card, propped up against the table's floral display where they were sure to see it. Then he escorted her outside. They had a short wait for a taxi, but before very long Laura found herself once more outside her apartment block.

'There's no need for you to come in,' she informed Quinn as he handed over some notes to the driver.

'My mother always told me it was good manners to see a lady to her door,' he informed her smoothly, climbing out and lending her a helping hand to alight.

He said nothing in the elevator, nor on the short walk to her door. There, he relieved her of her purse and found her key, opening the door and flicking on the light before standing back and allowing her to precede him. She hadn't expected him to follow her but, when she turned to thank him politely, he already had the door closed.

The calm action set her nerves dancing, and she watched him walk past her and into the lounge with a racing heart. She followed, dropping her coat on a chair.

'I really am rather tired, Quinn.' She remonstrated with him, hoping he would take the hint and leave.

He looked at her broodingly. 'Surely you can spare a cup of coffee?' he challenged, and, though she didn't want to, she knew it would be churlish to refuse.

'Very well. I'm out of fresh, though. It will have to be instant,' she told him as she crossed the lounge to the kitchen. It was a lie, but instant was quicker, which meant he would leave sooner.

'Instant is fine,' he told her, and with a sigh she checked the level of water in the kettle and switched it on. One cup of coffee and that was it.

She had set out two glazed mugs and was reaching for the jar of coffee when Quinn's arms slid around her. She let out a faint cry of alarm as his arms crossed over her wrist, pulling her back against him.

'Forget the coffee,' he declared huskily as she gasped, her hands automatically settling over his. An instant later the hot brush of his lips scalded the tender skin of her nape. 'That's not what I'm thirsting for right now.'

She shivered at the tingling pleasure which surged through her, arching her neck without thought to give him greater access. He took advantage of it and Laura groaned, trying to hang onto her sanity.

She licked dry lips agitatedly. 'Quinn. Please!' she moaned.

His hands moved, gliding upwards to capture her breasts, and helplessly she arched into his touch. 'I will. Dear God, you have no idea how I long to please you, darling,' he growled thickly.

Turning her in his arms, his hand snaked into her hair, angling her head for his kiss. It was devastating, plundering her mouth with a passion that was instantly arousing. Her arms went round his neck as she clung to him, kissing him back with an urgency that brought a whimper to the back of her throat. Quinn's hands glided down to her hips, then lower, clasping her bottom and raising her to the swell of his manhood. Her head fell back as her body contracted in response.

Quinn's voice was hot and heavy. 'No more games, Laura. This is what we both want, isn't it?'

Laura closed her eyes. She was so tired of fighting, and she wanted this. So very badly. She wouldn't think about tomorrow. Tonight, all that really mattered was that she loved this man, and she wanted to be with him. He wanted her, too. It wasn't about winning. It was about mutual passion. Mutual need.

'Yes,' she breathed. This had always been meant to happen. Nothing else mattered. Nothing. 'Make love to me. I want you so.'

With a growl of triumph Quinn reached down and picked her up.

CHAPTER NINE

THE bedroom was dark, save for the glow of artificial light filtering in from outside. Beside the bed, Quinn took his arm from beneath her legs, and she slid down his body until her feet touched the floor. They were breathing as if they had run a gruelling race, and she could hear his heart beating loudly. Or was it her own? She wasn't sure. All she knew was that need was rising inside her with volcanic intensity, driven on by drugging kisses.

Impatiently she kicked off her shoes and reached for his jacket, pushing it off his shoulders, and Quinn released her just long enough to shrug it off and toss it aside. Then he was pulling her to him once more, his hands finding the zip of her dress and dragging it down. His impatience was exciting, and she shuddered as his hands pushed the fabric aside and ran hotly up her spine. His touch on her body felt wonderful, and she was consumed with the need to touch him, too.

Her fingers stumbled over the buttons of his shirt, and with a groan she caught the fabric in both hands and tore it apart. She heard Quinn growl low in his throat, a sound of masculine satisfaction, and heat began to build up inside her as she was at last allowed the freedom to explore his magnificent body. His flesh burned under her hands, and his flat male nipples scraped against her palms. His head went back, air hissing in through his teeth, and the tense length of his throat was a lure she couldn't ignore. She swayed towards him, tongue darting out to explore the hollow at its base. He shuddered, and it set her heart racing to know she could make him react like this. Her lips followed, tracing a path emblazoned across his flesh by her tongue.

Somehow his shirt was gone, and Quinn's hands were on her shoulders, tugging the straps down, releasing the bodice from her swollen breasts. He held her away from him, and the dress became a green pool at her feet. Lips parted, she watched his eyes travel the length of her trembling body. Her nipples surged and her stomach fluttered, deepening the ache inside her. She longed for him to touch her and, as if he had heard her silent plea, his fingers trailed across the peak of her breast.

Laura cried out at the intense pleasure which shot through her body, lodging in the moist apex of her thighs. His thumb circled and teased until she moaned, her head falling back as she arched towards him. His hands claimed her, moulding her, holding her as his head dipped and he took her in his mouth. His tongue began doing magical things, turning her bones to water as it laved her straining nipple into almost painful hardness. When he began to suckle strongly, her knees buckled.

Quinn caught her, sweeping her up, laying her out on the bed and coming down beside her to deliver the same delicious torture to her other breast. Laura's fingers plunged into his hair, holding on tight as he drove her delirious with pleasure that bordered on pain. She moaned when he abandoned her turgid flesh, wanting more, but he ignored her. His lips were trailing a path down her body that set her heart racing and made it difficult to breathe. When his mouth brushed the skimpy lace of her panties, she stopped breathing altogether.

Oh, so slowly he drew the final piece of clothing away from her, and his lips followed. She had neither the will nor the desire to stop him when he parted her thighs and kissed her intimately. His tongue caressed her and deep inside the knot of pleasure began to tighten, drawing her higher and higher until, with a frantic cry of pleasure, she bucked and climaxed.

Lying in a glow of satisfaction, she watched as Quinn stood and quickly dispensed with the rest of his clothes. He looked magnificent. Totally male and proudly erect. She held out her arms to him, and he came down to her once more, taking her mouth in an erotic kiss that began to arouse her all over again. Yet she wanted to give him the same kind of pleasure he had given her and she pushed him onto his back, rising over him. She bit her lip as she concentrated on his pleasure. Her hands glided over the glistening planes of his chest, her nails scratching over his nipples, making him gasp, then continued on downwards. She found him, her fingers curling around the hard, velvety length of him, and air hissed through his teeth as he arched up from the bed. Her head lowered and she kissed him, but that was all he could take. With a growl he caught her hands and dragged her up, rolling over to pin her beneath him.

His hand traced a line from her shoulder to her hip. 'God, you're perfect,' he declared huskily, drawing her hand to his lips and kissing her palm.

She felt the gentle touch to her very soul, and her fingers curled. 'Love me,' she breathed, her free hand cupping his face and pulling him down to her.

They moved as one, all tangled limbs and broken sighs. It was glorious, as passion raged white-hot. They moaned under the lash of long, languorous caresses. Shuddered with each fevered, erotic kiss. Laura moved against him in ever increasing need for the satisfaction he denied her, torturing Quinn in her turn with bold sweeps of her hands. They pushed each other to the limit and beyond, until finally Quinn settled himself between her thighs and claimed her in one powerful thrust.

Laura cried out as above her Quinn froze, striving for control. But she did not want that, and her legs went around him as she arched to take him deeper inside her, moving against him until, with a groan, he was forced to join her. His thrusts became deeper, harder, and Laura held on tight as he propelled them out over the edge of sanity into the kaleidoscopic world of ecstasy. She cried out as the stunning climax took her, and there were tears of pure joy in her eyes as, seconds later, Quinn found his release.

Slowly they returned to the world, bodies sated, thrumming with indescribable pleasure. More than half asleep, she moaned as Quinn eased himself off her, then sighed with satisfaction as he drew her to him, settling her into the curve of his body. Her arm stole around him and, as sleep threatened to overcome her, she knew she was where she wanted to be.

'Quinn.' His name was a sighing breath on her lips.

His head tipped as he glanced down at her. His lips twisted. 'Damn you, Laura Maclane. Why did you have to be who you are?' he muttered under his breath.

She heard the sound of his voice from a long way away. 'Hmm? What did you say?' she murmured, frowning faintly, then sighed as his lips brushed her forehead.

'Nothing. Go to sleep, Laura,' he ordered gruffly, and, with the faintest of sighs, she did.

A familiar noise impinged on Laura's brain, drawing her reluctantly, but imperiously, from the comfortable world of sleep. Blinking owlishly, she took several seconds to realise she was hearing the unsubtle ringing of the telephone. She scrabbled for it with her hand, and was shocked to feel a band tighten around her waist.

Her eyes dropped to the sight of a male arm draped across her. Nerves leaping, she glanced over her shoulder and saw Quinn curled spoon fashion behind her. Memory returned with a wallop. Last night, she and Quinn had... Oh, God! She squeezed her eyes shut, but it didn't make reality fade away.

'You'd better answer that,' Quinn growled, reminding her that the telephone was still sounding out its shrill summons.

Swallowing hard, she reached for the receiver and jerked it to her ear. 'Hello?' Her voice sounded gravelly with sleep. She glanced at the clock. It was barely five in the morning.

'Laura? Thank goodness! I'm trying to find Quinn. Do you have any idea where he might be?' Maxine Harrington's frantic voice queried down the line.

Laura didn't bother asking why the woman would think she would know. There was alarm in the other woman's tone, and now was not the time to think about ridiculous things such as embarrassment. Maxine would not be ringing if something was not wrong.

'He's here, Mrs Harrington. I'll get him for you,' she said calmingly, turning to Quinn who was already sitting up. She handed him the receiver silently.

'Maxine?' he said, then frowned at the flow of words which followed. 'Calm down, Maxine. I can't help you if you don't calm down,' he ordered gently but firmly, raking a hand through his hair as he listened.

When he went still, Laura's heart sank. Dear God, what had happened? She got up, wincing as muscles protested. Grabbing her robe from behind the bathroom door, she slipped it on and turned back to the bed.

'Don't worry, Maxine. I'll be there as quickly as I can. Try to be calm. Philip is strong. He'll make it. Believe me,' Quinn was saying, setting her nerves jangling.

As soon as he set the receiver down, she went to him. 'What's happened to Philip?' she asked anxiously, watching as Quinn climbed unselfconsciously from the bed and began to retrieve his clothes.

'His car went out of control on an icy stretch of road. He's been taken to hospital.'

Laura's hand shot to her mouth. 'Oh, no!'

'Maxine heard about half an hour ago. She's been trying to reach me.' He picked up his shirt and grimaced at the sight. Laura flushed, recalling how impatient she had been to tear it off him last night. 'Do you have something of Alex's here?' he asked her.

'Of course not!' she denied in surprise, then caught her breath as she realised why he would assume she would have. After last night, it was a slap in the face to remember what he thought of her.

'Then this will have to do,' he said, slipping on the shirt, fastening what buttons remained then tucking the tails into his trousers. 'I told her I'd be at the hospital as soon as I could. There isn't time to go back to the hotel and change,' he decided, rubbing his hand over the night's growth of beard on his chin.

One part of her mind thought he looked damned sexy, but she ruthlessly pushed the thought aside. 'Is it serious? Is Philip likely to die?' She wanted to know, thinking how unreal it was that she had lost a father she had barely known, and was in danger of losing a half-brother too.

'I hope not. Maxine doesn't have too many details.'

Laura made an instant decision, knowing she could

not sit idly by here. 'I'm going with you,' she declared, crossing to the dressing table and pulling out clean underwear. From the closet she took jeans and a sweater.

'You aren't needed,' Quinn told her bluntly, and she paled, her chin rising defiantly.

'Perhaps not, but I'm going all the same!' Her expression dared him to argue.

He didn't. He merely reached for his jacket. 'I can't wait for you to get ready. I have to call a taxi.'

'No need,' she responded, jerking on her jeans over her panties then turning her back on him whilst she put on her bra and the sweater. 'I'll be ready before one could get here. It will be simpler to use my car.'

When she turned, Quinn was clearly debating whether to agree or not. Abruptly he nodded. 'I'll drive,' he declared, and a tiny smile curved her lips as she stamped her feet into her boots.

'OK,' she agreed. A flick of a brush through her hair and she was ready. 'You'll find the keys in the glass dish on the table by the front door,' she explained, and watched as Quinn strode into the other room.

Her eye was caught by the rumpled bed. She bit her lip at the blatant reminder, but there was no time now to think about how foolish she had been to sleep with him. She turned her back on the proof of her insanity and headed out of the door.

What followed was a nightmarish journey. The roads were treacherous after a night of severe frost, and although they wanted to go faster it would have been madness to do so. Quinn had told her that Philip had been taken to the nearest hospital to the site of the accident. It took several hours to reach it, by which time Laura was a bundle of nerves.

As Quinn pulled the car into the hospital parking area,

she couldn't help thinking how, in around twelve months, she had lost both her mother and her father. It didn't matter that Philip had been antagonistic when they met. He was her half-brother. She didn't think she could bear to lose another member of her family.

Quinn led the way inside. Getting directions from a nurse at the desk, he headed for the elevators, Laura hard on his heels like a faithful dog.

'I hope we're not too late,' she muttered as the doors closed and they were propelled upwards. 'God, I hate hospitals!'

Quinn shot her an odd glance. 'You didn't have to come. You still don't have to. You can wait in the restaurant if you'd prefer.'

She sent him a weak smile. 'No. I couldn't bear to wait alone. Poor Mrs Harrington. She must be feeling sick with worry.'

'Losing Alex nearly killed her. I don't know what she'll do if anything happens to Philip,' Quinn observed tersely, and Laura shivered.

'I know how she feels,' she said with feeling, and he frowned at her.

'How can you? Alex wasn't your husband. Philip isn't your son.'

If he'd slapped her he couldn't have hurt her more. It was on the tip of her tongue to say no, one was her father and the other her half-brother, but she kept silent by sheer effort of will. 'It's possible to empathise. I've lost both my parents, so I know how it feels to lose those you love,' she told him coldly, and stepped out ahead of him when the door opened.

Quinn caught her gently by the arm. 'I'm sorry,' he said. 'That was uncalled for.'

'Yes, it was,' she agreed stonily, and he sighed.

'Come on, let's find Maxine. By now she'll be frantic.'

They found her in Intensive Care, sitting beside the motionless body of her son. A doctor stood at her side, talking to her quietly. Philip was hitched up to all sorts of machines that flashed and beeped. He was as pale as the sheets on his bed. Maxine glanced round as they entered the room, her relief patent as she stood up.

'Oh, Quinn!' she gasped in a wobbly voice, and was instantly enveloped in the warmth of his arms. She only allowed herself a small bout of weeping before squaring her shoulders and taking a deep breath. That was when she really noticed Laura for the first time. 'Laura?' she queried in surprise.

'I made Quinn bring me. I hope you don't mind,' Laura explained, squeezing her arm comfortingly. 'Is there anything I can do, Mrs Harrington?'

Maxine shook her head, biting her lip until she was able to speak. 'There's not much anyone can do until Stella gets here.'

Laura didn't get the connection, but Quinn clearly did. 'They're going to have to operate?' he asked at once, and Maxine nodded.

'There's a blood clot on his brain, and it's getting worse. They only had so much of the right blood, and they used that when they operated before,' she explained, turning to where the doctor hovered nearby.

'We've radioed out for more, but this blood group is very rare. We don't know where it will have to come from, or if we'll have to ask for donations from registered donors. It could take hours to get here,' the doctor enlarged as he joined them.

'I've sent for Stella, and she's on her way. They'll operate as soon as she gets here and donates some blood.

But he's getting worse, Quinn. I just know I'm going to lose him!' Maxine exclaimed, pressing a hand over her mouth to hold back her anguish.

Laura had gone utterly still as she listened. She had never thought that her secret would be revealed in this manner. It wasn't the way she would have chosen, but she knew she could not stand by when it was in her power to help.

'How long will it take Stella to get here?' she asked in a scratchy voice, and Maxine and Quinn turned to face her.

'Ian was hopeful he could make the trip in two hours, and that was almost an hour ago now,' Maxine responded, glancing at her watch.

'And that's all they're waiting for? For Stella to get here and give blood?' She sought confirmation.

'That's all,' the doctor confirmed. 'We're ready to go the minute she arrives.'

Laura took a deep breath, knowing she was about to drop a bombshell that would have repercussions she couldn't even imagine. 'Perhaps there isn't any need to wait. You may be able to use my blood,' she said clearly, and it felt as if the whole room held its breath. It was the doctor who reacted first.

'You have the same type blood?' he exclaimed in surprise, and Laura didn't dare look at Quinn. She kept her eyes on Maxine, silently begging her understanding.

'It's possible, yes.'

His expression cleared miraculously. 'Then come this way and let's get you typed right away!' he declared, taking her arm as if he feared she might disappear and urging her towards the door.

There she paused and glanced back at two stunned expressions. 'I'll explain later,' she promised, and gasped aloud as Quinn had to reach out quickly to catch Maxine's collapsing body. 'Oh, my God!'

Quinn flashed a glittering look at her over his shoulder. 'Go. I'll take care of her. She's fainted, that's all.'

Laura reluctantly allowed herself to be led away to another room where her blood was typed and, as she expected, proved a perfect match. Soon she was lying on a bed, and her thoughts turned to Maxine. She hoped Quinn was right, and that it was nothing more serious than a faint. If anything worse happened, she would never forgive herself.

It seemed to take for ever to give the maximum allowance of blood, and then she was left alone with a cup of tea and a cookie to recover. She drank the tea, then dozed for a bit. It was a small sound which stirred her, and she opened her eyes to find Maxine at the foot of the bed. The woman looked pale, but composed.

'Philip?' Laura asked at once, coming up on her elbow.

'They're operating now...thanks to you,' Maxine said gently, and all at once Laura became self-conscious, aware that she had a lot of explaining to do.

'I guess you want to ask me some questions,' she said uneasily, but much to her surprise the other woman shook her head.

'I see it now, the thing that was puzzling me. It's your eyes. You have Alex's eyes.'

Laura licked her lips, heart pounding anxiously. 'I'm his daughter,' she said flatly, and wasn't prepared for the way Maxine's lips twitched in a faint smile.

'I guessed as much,' she said dryly as she came round to sit on the edge of the bed. 'Now you're wondering why I'm not shocked or angry,' she added, confusing Laura with her response.

'Why aren't you?' she asked curiously.

Maxine studied her folded hands, and sighed. 'Because I know my husband was never unfaithful to me. I also know there was someone else before he met me. Oh, he never told me, but a woman knows these things. Am I right in thinking she was your mother?'

Laura's fingers rose to where her locket sat beneath her sweater. 'They had an affair when they were at university. She never told Alexander about me, or me about him. Whenever I asked about my father, she always said there was nothing to tell. It wasn't until she died that I found out who he was. She had me tell him about her death and he realised who I must be at once. I loved her very much, but I'll never understand why she did what she did.'

A tiny frown pleated Maxine's brow. 'She never married?'

'No.'

'She must have loved him very much,' Maxine said gently, and Laura frowned.

'I like to think so, but... To keep us from knowing each other? It's so extreme.'

'Love makes people do strange things. Like leaving an apparent stranger money in your will,' Maxine declared wryly, bringing colour to Laura's cheeks.

'Believe me, I never expected to be left any money when Alexander died,' she said, wanting to get that out of the way.

'But it's the kind of thing Alex would do. I know it would have hurt him not to have known you as a child. I'm sure, had he known about you, he would have played a much bigger part in your life. But as that could not be he would have made certain you had what was yours by right as his daughter,' she declared, bringing a lump of emotion to Laura's throat.

'I loved him, you know. I didn't know him long, but I did love him.'

Maxine patted her hand. 'I'm sure you did. Alex was an easy man to love.'

Laura nodded, but she couldn't help frowning at the other woman. 'You don't seem to mind the fact of me,' she said, pleased yet undeniably puzzled.

Maxine did not attempt to make light of it. 'I admit to being shocked. How could I not be? But you are Alex's daughter. I asked myself how I would have felt had I known of your existence before I married him. The answer was simple. I loved Alex. I would willingly have accepted you as my stepdaughter. If I could do it then, I can do it now. The fact that you're a grown woman doesn't change anything. Who knows? It might even make it easier. Laura, the past is out of our control. All we have is the present. You are who you are. It will take some getting used to, and a great deal of explaining. Which reminds me. I am curious to know why neither of you thought fit to tell me who you were.'

Laura pulled a face because, after all that had happened, the reason sounded rather lame. 'Alexander was worried about your health. He feared what the shock might do.'

'That sounds like Alex. He never would accept that I'm stronger than I look.'

Laura laughed, because the truth was right before her. 'He was awfully careful of you. That's why I couldn't say anything either, after he died. I wanted to. I wanted to meet my half-brother and sister, but I didn't want to harm you in the process. That's why I had Jonathan take me with him, so that I could get to know you and see for myself how you would take the news.'

Maxine's brows rose. 'Yet you left without telling me. Why?'

Colour flooded into Laura's cheeks. 'That had nothing to do with you. It was...something altogether different,' she said vaguely.

'Quinn does have that effect on people,' Maxine said dryly, and Laura caught her breath.

'I didn't say it was Quinn,' she denied hastily as Maxine rose to her feet.

'My dear, you didn't have to. Seeing you two together is like walking into an electrical storm. It's quite breathtaking, believe me. Now, you must rest. We'll talk later when we have more time. Oh, and there is just one thing.'

'Yes?'

'Call me Maxine. Mrs Harrington is far too formal to call someone you're related to, even if it is only by marriage,' she declared, and left Laura in a state of pleasant astonishment.

Never in her wildest imaginings had she dreamt she would be accepted so readily. She knew it was because Maxine Harrington was an exceptional woman. Thank God for it. She felt caught between laughter and tears. It was such a relief to be freed from the restraints her fears had put upon her. No longer did she have to watch her words. The secret was out.

She sobered. The secret might be out, but that was the least of her worries. She had no idea how Stella would take the news. And Quinn... She recalled his expression. He would be furious. She had made a fool of him, and she knew in her bones that he would never forgive her for it. Part of her life might suddenly have become easier, but there was another part that had just got worse.

She lay back, closing her eyes. What she and Quinn had shared last night had been wonderful. Everything she had ever expected it would be. But it hadn't suddenly made him love her. It had been an incredible experience and she would never forget it, but it would never happen again. An affair was out of the question. Not that that was likely. Because Quinn knew the truth now, and the truth changed everything between them.

She sighed again. He had never loved her, but after this how would he feel?

Philip's room was empty when she finally returned to it. Sitting down, she glanced through a magazine someone had left on the table, but it couldn't hold her interest. She paced for a bit after that, but she was staring out of the window at an early morning sky laden with snow when something told her she was not alone. She turned. Quinn stood framed in the doorway. His expression was as remote and forbidding as she had ever seen it and she shivered, folding her arms protectively around her.

'Congratulations,' he drawled chillingly. 'Not many people have succeeded in making a fool of me, but you did it with style. Were you ever going to tell me the truth?'

His remoteness was hardly encouraging and she winced, squaring her shoulders, prepared to tell the truth yet knowing it was not going to be easy. 'Eventually everyone would have known, but Maxine had to be told first. That was only fair.'

'Fair!' he exploded, closing the gap between them in angry strides which brought him within a foot of her. 'Did you think it was fair to let me believe you were Alex's mistress when you were actually his daughter?'

She flinched in the face of his rage but held her ground, for he was not without blame himself.

'I only let you believe what you wanted to believe,' she pointed out defensively.

The ice in his eyes was inches thick. 'You lied to me,' he accused furiously, and her chin came up. There was absolutely no way she was taking all the blame.

'You jumped to conclusions. You wanted to think the worst of me.'

His jaw clenched with the violence of his anger. 'Did that mean you had to do your best to convince me I was right, rather than tell me I was wrong?' he challenged caustically.

'Come on, Quinn, we both know you wouldn't have believed me,' she scoffed, and he sent her a withering look.

'You knew more than I did. You never gave me the chance to decide for myself. Perhaps I would have believed you, but we'll never know now, will we?'

In a pig's eye they didn't know! 'For goodness' sake, you know you would never have believed me because you don't trust women,' she insisted firmly, refusing to cower.

'Who says I don't?' he shot back, and that gave her pause.

'Caroline. She said you didn't trust women after Tonia let you down. Isn't it true?' she asked uncertainly, and those beautiful blue eyes flashed derisively.

'Maybe it is, and maybe it isn't, but, hell, sweetheart, you certainly proved I couldn't trust *you!*'

At that a spark of anger ignited inside her. 'Why does that rankle? You didn't want to trust me!' she exclaimed wrathfully, and he raised one eyebrow questioningly.

'Didn't I?' he taunted softly.

Taken aback, Laura caught her breath. 'And just what is that supposed to mean?'

'It means *darling,* that even if you couldn't have told me who you were you should have told me who you weren't!' he said tautly.

She looked away, because he had a point. She should have made the effort to convince him he was wrong. However, she was too angry herself now to admit it. 'You were having too much fun thinking the worst of me,' she retorted, and he drew in an angry breath.

'And what about you? Were you having fun? Did you enjoy the joke?' he charged dangerously, and she glared at him.

'As it happens, yes, I did,' she told him rashly, then shivered at the look in his eyes. There was a warning there, but she ignored it. 'So is that it? Have you finished?'

Quinn stared at her for a long moment, then laughed grimly. 'Not quite.' He reached into his jacket pocket and produced a long flat box which he held out to her.

'What is it?' she asked suspiciously.

'Open it and see,' he suggested mockingly, watching her narrowly.

She didn't really want to, but curiosity got the better of her. With faintly trembling fingers she took the box and opened it. Her breath caught audibly as she stared down at the diamond and sapphire necklace which sparkled up at her from a bed of black silk. She couldn't seem to take her eyes off it, and stood transfixed.

'Do you like it? It's for you. Payment for last night. It was expensive, but you were worth every penny of it!' he declared insolently, and Laura flinched as if he had struck her, the colour draining from her face.

'You bastard!' she whispered through a painfully tight throat.

A nerve ticked in his jaw as he pulled something else from his pocket. 'Your car keys. You'll need them to get home.' When she didn't reach out and take them, he tossed them on the bed. 'Goodbye, Laura. It's been…interesting knowing you,' he added mockingly, then turned on his heel and walked from the room.

Laura hadn't thought it was possible to hurt so much. Hate rose up inside her on the wings of a volcanic rage. How dared he? Damn him. How dared he do that to her? With a groan of disgust, she flung the box and its glittering contents at the wall. The necklace fell out and lay staring up at her mockingly. Stricken, she turned her back on it.

She had known he didn't love her, but to offer her payment… It made everything that they had shared last night unclean. She had given herself with love, damn it, even if he had not. He had turned something wonderful into something ugly. She would never forgive him for that. Never.

If only she could make him pay!

She didn't know how, but she would think of something. Something to make him hurt as she was hurting. She turned, staring at the necklace, lips pressed tight together to still their trembling. There was at least one thing she could do. With determination, she walked over to the necklace and picked it up, setting it back in the box and closing the lid so she didn't have to look at it. She would take the damn thing and fling it in his face. And while she was at it she would tell him just exactly how much she hated, loathed and despised him!

CHAPTER TEN

'LAURA!'

Anya Kovacs' sharp tone pierced Laura's preoccupation. She came to with a start and glanced up at her friend and partner who stood, hands on hips, before her desk.

'Yes? What is it?'

Anya looked as if she didn't know whether to be angry or despairing. 'I've been talking to you for the last ten minutes, and you just drifted off!' she complained frustratedly, and Laura flushed. That had been happening all day.

'Sorry,' she said. 'What were we talking about?'

With a sigh, Anya propped herself on the corner of the desk and eyed her friend solemnly. 'Laura, this is not like you. What's going on?' she asked curiously, then some thought obviously struck her because her eyes lit up. 'I know! It's a man, isn't it? You've finally met Mr Right!' she exclaimed in delight, and no little amusement.

Laura scowled. 'Mr Right turned out to be Mr Wrong,' she snapped, and Anya's eyes became saucers.

'Come on, then. Tell me all the gory details,' she urged salaciously, but Laura didn't smile.

'Sorry, but I can't,' she said with a grimace, and her friend instantly stopped joking around.

'Then...you really did meet Mr Right?'

Laura pursed her lips and raised a diffident shoulder. 'I'd rather not talk about it now.' It was too raw. What

174

Quinn had done was like an open wound festering inside her.

Anya was all concern. 'Gosh, I'm sorry, Laura. It hurts, huh?' she said, pulling a pained face.

'And then some,' was all Laura was prepared to admit. 'Don't you have somewhere to be?' she prompted, and her friend glanced at the clock and jumped to her feet.

'You're right, I'd better get a move on. I'm going to go straight home after the meeting, unless you need me back here for anything?'

Laura shook her head. 'No, there's nothing urgent. We'll get together on that new client tomorrow.'

Anya bustled about for a while getting her things together, then departed with a wave. Left alone in the studio—Felix having taken the afternoon off—Laura sat back in her seat and closed her eyes tiredly. She had hardly slept the last few nights, and it was taking its toll.

Had it really been only two days ago? It seemed for ever. There had been no opportunity to confront Quinn, and she could not have done so at the hospital, anyway. It would have been out of place. So, hiding her hurt, she had stayed with Maxine until the other woman had insisted she go home while the conditions were still good. By that time Philip was back in ICU and doing well. She had not seen Quinn again before she left.

Her determination to return the necklace had not faded, but the means had not presented itself. She had found out from Jonathan where Quinn generally stayed when he was in town, but he had booked out of the hotel. This morning, she had managed to get hold of his home telephone number, but the woman who'd answered had said she was the cleaner and that Mr Mannion was away. That might or might not be true but to drive out to

Maine, even supposing she managed to get his address, would be a waste of time if he really was away, and not just incommunicado.

Frustrated at all turns, she had had to put her anger on hold.

Sighing, she returned to the swags of material she was thinking of using for her current commission. She worked steadily for the rest of the afternoon, and long after she heard the other occupants of her floor lock up and leave for the day. She was trying to decide between two shades of pink when she heard the studio door open. She looked up automatically, and froze when she saw who her visitor was.

For a second she could only sit and stare as Quinn calmly closed the door behind him and crossed the floor towards her desk. He was dressed as she had first seen him, in leather jacket, sweater and jeans, and was as devastatingly handsome as ever. Her heart started racing at a sickening pace and she shot to her feet, hands curling into fists where they lay on the desktop.

'What are you doing here?' she demanded tersely. 'Get out!'

He didn't pause in his stride. 'Not until I've said what I came to say,' he refused coolly, and anger became a hot ball in her stomach.

'You have nothing to say that I want to hear. Get out, or I'll call the police and have you arrested for trespass!' she declared, reaching for the receiver, but Quinn got there before her and moved the phone beyond her reach.

He looked at her steadily, a nerve ticking in his jaw a sure sign of tension. 'Just hear me out, Laura,' he urged, holding her gaze.

Folding her arms, she tossed her head. 'Why should I?'

He drew in a long breath and straightened up, tucking his hands into the pockets of his jeans. 'Because I came here to apologise,' he told her gruffly, taking her completely by surprise.

Her jaw dropped. She hadn't expected that, and it infuriated her that she had been outmanoeuvred. She had needed her anger to combat the hurt. She had wanted to hurt him, but he had jerked the rug out from under her and left her floundering.

'Oh, really?' she said frostily, trying to recover lost ground.

Something flashed in his eyes and was instantly hidden. 'I'm sorry for what happened the other day. I was shocked and angry, but that was no excuse for the way I behaved,' he said with determination.

'No, it wasn't,' she agreed in a strangled voice. A bubble of emotion began expanding in her chest and she couldn't seem to control it. She didn't know whether it was anger or hurt.

Quinn sighed. 'I didn't mean it.'

Her chin had an alarming tendency to wobble, and she pressed her lips together tightly to hide it. 'Which part?'

He studied the toe of his boot for a moment, then met her eyes stoically. 'The bit about the necklace,' he admitted ruefully, and she caught her breath. 'You are worth every penny of it, just like I said, but not for the reason I made you think.'

Pain lanced through her at the unwelcome reminder, and colour stormed into her cheeks. 'You sounded like you meant it exactly as you said it,' she choked out.

He dragged a hand through his hair. 'I know. I was angry. You had made a fool of me, and...I thought I meant it too. But I knew that I had hurt you, and I couldn't live with myself if I left you believing the lie.'

Pride had her chin lifting. 'You didn't hurt me!' she denied instantly, and he looked at her wryly.

'Yes, I did,' he said regretfully, and she bit her lip and looked away.

'Well, you've apologised now, so you can go with a clear conscience.'

Quinn shifted his weight more comfortably. 'Not yet. Not until I've told you why I reacted as I did.'

She glanced back, frowning. 'You told me why.'

'Not all of it,' he corrected her with a shake of his head. 'You deserve to hear everything. But first I have to ask you something. Why do you think I slept with you that night?'

She gasped. How dared he ask her that? 'I'd rather not talk about it. In fact, I'd rather you just left,' she told him bluntly.

Quinn folded his arms to show he was here to stay. 'Just answer the question, Laura,' he insisted, and she glared at him.

Humiliated colour washed her cheeks. 'Damn you! You did it to win the game, of course! You said you would have me, and you did!' she exclaimed in disgust.

'I know what I said, but I didn't make love to you to win a game,' Quinn countered, and anger rose to choke her.

'Liar! There was no other reason!'

Faint colour entered his cheeks at her claim. 'Maybe not for you, but there was for me. There was also need. I needed you. Wanting you was driving me out of my mind, and I lost the battle.'

Laura shook her head in confusion. He was making no sense. 'What battle?'

'The one I was waging with myself,' he admitted huskily. 'If you hadn't said yes that night, I would have given you the necklace and told you you had won, because my need for you was too great.'

Her throat closed over. She knew all about need. She had needed him, too, but that was different. 'Quinn, I...'

'I fell in love with you on sight, Laura Maclane, and that is God's honest truth.'

Quinn's declaration was so stunning, her arms fell to her sides and her lips parted on a sharp intake of breath.

'What did you say?' she asked in disbelief, sure she must have misheard him.

Quinn gritted his teeth. 'I said I fell in love with you. You were the most beautiful woman I had ever met. Touching you was like being licked by flame. I felt you to my soul.'

Laura blinked and sat down abruptly. He *had* said it. Quinn loved her. It was incredible. Unbelievable. She pressed a hand to her heart. She knew she should say something, but words wouldn't come. Then Quinn turned away, walking to a nearby window and staring out into the darkness.

'I don't expect this to change anything between us. I'm telling you because I believe you have a right to know why I was so angry. It wasn't just because you made a fool of me, you see. I believed you were Alex's mistress, and to be attracted to you was not something I was proud of. In fact, I disgusted myself. You were so blatant, so unashamed, I couldn't believe I could want you so much. So I hid my feelings behind the contempt I had for you but, as you know, you were impossible to ignore.

'You had me so I didn't know whether I was coming or going. I made love to you because it was as necessary to me as breathing. Then Philip had his accident...' He took a deep breath before going on. 'To discover that everything you had said and done had been a big lie was more than I could handle at the time. I was angry and I struck out at you. Which was wrong because you had no way of knowing how I felt about you,' he finished, glancing round at her sombrely.

Laura closed her eyes as her anger seemed just to melt away. Seeing her actions from Quinn's point of view was a salutary lesson. He had loved her all that time, and there was no comfort in telling herself she had not known. She hadn't had to feed his bad opinion. She could have tried to convince him differently right from the outset. She had known he was wrong, but he had only known what she told him. No wonder he had been furious.

Her heart contracted. He hadn't had to tell her any of this, but he had chosen to because he knew he had hurt her. It was only fair that she should tell him why she had been so hurt.

'That was all I came to say. I won't take up any more of your time.' Quinn's husky words brought her eyes open in a hurry to see him walking away from her. He was leaving, and she knew he would not be back. She could not allow that to happen.

'Wait!' she called out hastily, and he paused mid-stride. 'Don't you want to know why I slept with you?' she charged in a shaky voice, and he turned towards her, expression guarded.

'You don't have to do this,' he warned, visibly bracing himself, and the faintest of smiles curved itself about her lips.

'Oh, yes, I do. You see, I fell in love with you on sight, too,' she confessed quietly, and saw him tense with shock. 'I didn't realise it at the time. Your eyes were so blue, I felt like I was drowning in them. I knew I was attracted to you, for nobody else had ever made me feel the way you did. It was because I was so angry with you that I didn't realise it was love I felt.'

She smiled wryly. 'We're more alike than you know. You see, I was hiding too. I couldn't let you see that I was attracted to someone who felt the way you did. When I realised I had fallen in love with you, I was even more worried. I tried to keep you at arm's length, but it didn't work.'

'It never would,' Quinn said, his voice gravelly with the depth of his emotion, but his eyes were blazing. 'We wanted each other too much. I still do want you. I can't imagine the wanting ever going away,' he added huskily, and her heart turned over.

Their eyes met and the proof was there, just below the surface, simmering away. The sounds of the world outside faded away. Suddenly the room was resounding with that crackling electricity they generated whenever they were together, only now it was stronger than before, because it abounded with love.

Laura drew in a shaky breath. 'If I tell you I love you now, will you believe me?' she asked, and Quinn threw back his head and laughed out loud. A purely masculine sound of pleasure.

He looked so relaxed, so very much the Quinn she had always wanted to know, that her heart felt full to overflowing. 'Is that a yes or a no?' she asked sardonically, and he looked at her with such an expression in his wonderful blue eyes, it made her want to laugh and cry all at the same time.

He closed the space between them in two strides, drawing her to her feet and into his arms. Lifting a visibly trembling hand, he stroked her cheek. 'That, darling Laura, is most definitely a yes,' he said thickly, and, closing his eyes, he rested his forehead against hers and drew in a deep breath. 'Does this mean you forgive me?'

'I'll forgive you if you forgive me,' she offered gently, and he groaned.

'You have a generous heart, Laura Maclane. It's one of the reasons I love you so damned much!'

'You were going to walk away,' she said softly, and he sighed.

'The last thing I wanted to do was hurt you any more than I had,' he confessed.

Laura glanced down, running a hand over his heart. 'I was going to throw that necklace back in your face, with a few choice words,' she revealed teasingly, and he captured her hand, bringing it up to press a kiss into her palm.

'I'll take it back and change it. The next necklace I give you will most definitely be given with love. Because I do love you, sweetheart, hard as it is to believe.'

'No, it isn't, it's easy. But I don't mind if you want to keep proving it to me. In fact...'

The rest died under the soft brush of his lips, and she smiled and kissed him back. There was still a lot of explaining to do but, as someone had once said so memorably, tomorrow was another day.

EPILOGUE

LAURA looked out at the silently falling snow and felt a smile coming on. She had done a lot of smiling in the blissful six months she had been married to Quinn. Now it was Christmas again, and all the family were gathered together to celebrate it. This time it truly was a family gathering. Her family. She could see the whole sweep of it reflected in the glass of the window, and glanced over her shoulder at the cosy scene.

Philip, completely recovered from his accident, was stretched out on the carpet playing a game with Tom and Ellie, whilst Stella sat in the curve of Ian's arm, laughing as she offered unwanted advice to her brother. From her chair by the fire, Maxine smiled fondly at her children, her young grandson nestling in her lap, fast asleep.

Caroline and Jonathan were there too, looking so happy it caused Laura's smile to deepen. They had been married for six weeks and the honeymoon didn't show any signs of being over. She didn't think it ever would end. If ever two people seemed right for each other, then it was these two.

Suddenly Tom whooped in triumph, as Philip conceded defeat.

'You're too good for me, Tom,' he admitted, climbing to his feet. Catching sight of Laura watching him, he grinned and winked, and she laughed.

It warmed her how whole-heartedly she had been accepted into the family. She had expected resistance from her brother and sister—she thought of them that way now—but they had surprised her. From the moment they realised how she had helped save Philip's life, their attitude had changed. Their antagonism had come from a mixture of grief for the loss of their father, and the need to protect their mother. Discovering she was not their father's mistress, but their own half-sister, had come as a shock. Yet that shock had been tempered by gratitude. Stella had said it herself. How could she resent the existence of someone who had helped her brother?

The angry young man and woman of a year ago had vanished, never to return. True, they had been awkward with each other at the start, careful not to say the wrong thing, but from stilted beginnings a true affection had grown. Now it was hard to imagine there had ever been a time when they had not got on.

It was everything Laura had ever wanted, to be part of her family.

She started as a pair of strong arms slipped around her, pulling her back against a powerful male body, then relaxed into the familiar hold.

'You're wearing that look again,' Quinn murmured, his lips brushing her neck and sending shivers of pleasure down her spine.

Sighing, she folded her hands over his and tipped her head to ease his access. 'Mmm…what look is that?' she asked huskily.

'The one that says life couldn't get any better than this.'

Lifting a hand, she softly caressed his cheek. 'It's true. I have my family, and I have you. What more could I want?'

Quinn caught her hand and pressed a kiss to her palm, folding her fingers over the spot protectively.

'Uh-oh!' A young voice broke into their cocoon of happiness. 'Uncle Quinn and Aunty Laura are getting all soppy again!' Ellie declared disgustedly, arms akimbo and wearing a furious frown.

The whole room dissolved into laughter and, not understanding why, the little girl went to her mother and climbed up onto her lap for instant comfort. Meanwhile, Quinn's blue eyes danced as he glanced down at his wife.

'She thinks we're mad,' he grinned, and Laura smiled back at him with all her love.

'Well, I am absolutely crazy about you,' she confessed.

'I'm more than a little nuts about you, too,' Quinn agreed lightly, tightening his hold. 'When you get right down to it, we deserve each other.'

'A perfect match.'

'Do you think there's any chance they'll go to bed early?' Quinn asked, watching his nephew and niece playing with seemingly boundless energy.

'I wouldn't count on it,' Laura remarked wryly. 'It's Christmas Eve, remember. But if you're good I'll let you unwrap one present later,' she promised huskily, and felt his immediate response.

'Do I get to choose which one?'

Turning in his arms, she reached up to plant a swift kiss on his lips. 'Nope. I choose, but I promise you won't be disappointed,' she added with a sultry look, before slipping out of his arms and going to join the rest of the family.

Laughing, Quinn followed, knowing she was right. He wouldn't be disappointed by this woman. Intrigued, certainly. Surprised, constantly. Delighted, inevitably, but never, ever disappointed.

*M*akes
any time
special

Enjoy a romantic novel from
Mills & Boon®

Presents™ *Enchanted*™ *Temptation*®

Historical Romance™ *Medical Romance*™

MILLS & BOON®

Next Month's Romance Titles

$\heartsuit$

Each month you can choose from a wide variety of romance novels from Mills & Boon®. Below are the new titles to look out for next month from the Presents™ and Enchanted™ series.

Presents™

TO WOO A WIFE	Carole Mortimer
CONTRACT BABY	Lynne Graham
IN BED WITH THE BOSS	Susan Napier
SURRENDER TO SEDUCTION	Robyn Donald
OUTBACK MISTRESS	Lindsay Armstrong
THE SECRET DAUGHTER	Catherine Spencer
THE MARRIAGE ASSIGNMENT	Alison Kelly
WIFE BY AGREEMENT	Kim Lawrence

Enchanted™

BE MY GIRL!	Lucy Gordon
LONESOME COWBOY	Debbie Macomber
A SUITABLE GROOM	Liz Fielding
NEW YEAR...NEW FAMILY	Grace Green
OUTBACK HUSBAND	Jessica Hart
MAKE-BELIEVE MOTHER	Pamela Bauer & Judy Kaye
OH, BABY!	Lauryn Chandler
FOLLOW THAT GROOM!	Christie Ridgway

On sale from 8th January 1999

H1 9812

Available at most branches of WH Smith, Tesco, Asda, Martins, Borders and all good paperback bookshops

MILLS & BOON®

Medical Romance™

COMING NEXT MONTH

SARAH'S GIFT by Caroline Anderson
Audley Memorial Hospital

Having lost her own family, Sarah loved having Matt Ryan
and his little girl, Emily, living with her while they were in
England. She didn't know that Matt had an inestimable
gift for her...

POTENTIAL DADDY by Lucy Clark

Kathryn wasn't sure she liked the professional Jack—brilliant
and arrogant—but his private side was a revelation. He'd
make the perfect father, but who would he choose as the
mother of his potential children?

LET TOMORROW COME by Rebecca Lang

Gerard came to Jan's help when she most needed it, but she
found it so hard to trust, she was sure he'd have a hidden
agenda. How could he convince her that he hadn't?

THE PATIENT MAN by Margaret O'Neill

Harry Paradine knew if he was patient enough that the right
woman would come along. When she finally did, he found
Emily Prince less than trustful—but why?

*Available at most branches of WH Smith, Tesco, Asda,
Martins, Borders, Easons, Volume One/James Thin
and most good paperback bookshops*

MILLS & BOON®

Makes any time special™

Bestselling themed romances brought back to you by popular demand

Each month By Request brings you three full-length novels in one beautiful volume featuring the best of the best.

So if you missed a favourite Romance the first time around, here is your chance to relive the magic from some of our most popular authors.

**Look out for
Blind Passions in January 1999
featuring Miranda Lee,
Rebecca Winters and Emma Goldrick**

*Available at most branches of WH Smith, Tesco, Asda,
Martins, Borders, Easons, Volume One/James Thin
and most good paperback bookshops*

We are giving away a year's supply of Mills & Boon® books to the five lucky winners of our latest competition. Simply match the six film stars to the films in which they appeared, complete the coupon overleaf and send this entire page to us by 30th June 1999. The first five correct entries will each win a year's subscription to the Mills & Boon series of their choice. What could be easier?

CABARET	___	GONE WITH THE WIND ___
ROCKY	___	SMOKEY & THE BANDIT ___
PRETTY WOMAN	___	GHOST ___

C8L

Please turn over for details of how to enter ➜

HOW TO ENTER

There are six famous faces and a list of six films overleaf. Each of the famous faces starred in one of the films listed and all you have to do is match them up!

As you match each one, write the number of the actor or actress who starred in each film in the space provided. When you have matched them all, fill in the coupon below, pop this page in an envelope and post it today. Don't forget you could win a year's supply of Mills & Boon® books—you don't even need to pay for a stamp!

Mills & Boon Hollywood Heroes Competition
FREEPOST CN81, Croydon, Surrey, CR9 3WZ
EIRE readers: (please affix stamp) PO Box 4546, Dublin 24.

Please tick the series you would like to receive if you are one of the lucky winners

Presents™ ❑   Enchanted™ ❑   Historical Romance™ ❑

Medical Romance™ ❑   Temptation® ❑

Are you a Reader Service™ subscriber?   Yes ❑   No ❑

Ms/Mrs/Miss/Mr ....Initials ....
(BLOCK CAPITALS PLEASE)

Surname...

Address ....

....

....Postcode...........................

(I am over 18 years of age)   C8L

Closing date for entries is 30th June 1999. One entry per household. Free subscriptions are for four books per month. Competition open to residents of the UK and Ireland only. As a result of this application, you may receive further offers from Harlequin Mills & Boon and other carefully selected companies. If you would prefer not to share in this opportunity please write to The Data Manager at the address shown above.

Mills & Boon is a registered trademark of
Harlequin Mills & Boon Ltd.